IT HAPPENED ALONG THE HAINES

"GOLD RUSH ALASKA" HIGHWAY:

Tales of Intrigue from Mosquito Lake to Porcupine Creek, Alaska

DAVID VOTH

CONTENTS

OVER THE HAINES HIGHWAY

Anne had been running for a long time. She had to stop, but stopping would mean that it had happened, that it was real. If she could just keep running, the dizziness and the pain would keep her in that place where nothing was real except the throbbing beat of pain in her feet.

But it was no use. When she had started, the bright moon was just peaking out over the mountains across from the Chilkat River. Now the moon beat down from directly above, lighting the two-track dirt path to Klukwan from Haines. She had been keeping to the more established footpath that had been created centuries ago, with the less established second tire track from automobile traffic becoming harder and harder to see. Stopped and bent over, the full impact of the strain she had imposed upon her body wretched her to her knees. There was a burning fire in her lungs, and a flat wobbling throb in her limbs. And one other new pain. The worst of all. The pain that now reminded her that she was no longer a virgin. Now she realized, she could not run from that pain. It was no use. She was now ruined. No good. And her life was over.

Looking about, Anne recognized her night surroundings. She had run halfway to Klukwan without stopping. The Dakhéen River was across from the open area she now stood upon and the trademark cold September wind associated with that spot on the river was chilling her rapidly since she had stopped moving. Her neck was particularly cold where she had cut her hair short to look like the flapper girls in the magazine. The magazine sent by the Devil. If only she had never seen that picture…

Anne heard herself sobbing again, but the tears did not come. She had run out of tears hours ago and miles away. Now what could she do? Crawling to the riverbank she sucked at cold silt-filled water, scooping large gulps with her shaking hands. Rolling on her back, Anne let the fluid trickle down her middle insides, starting a series of quaking shivers as her body tried in vain to create heat to counteract the freezing water now sloshing inside. Maybe she would die. No, she had to die. That was it. It was time for her to die. What could she do?

On her back, the cold stars comforted her. They were the same. They didn't care that she was now ruined. They were happy, shiny, not like Mathew. Oh, Mathew! Oh how I love you.

"I'm so sorry!" Anne said out loud to the roar of the black river. "I'm sorry," she whispered.

The entire night came rushing back in her head and in her loins, nauseating her as she also saw Mathew in her mind, as if he were witnessing it all. It had started so good, so fun. Anne's best friend Jill cut her hair to match the magazine pictures. She picked and wore her liveliest dress for an evening of imagination and fun with her boyfriend. She was spectacular in grandmother's full-length mirror. Grandmother even let her borrow the bright yellow stone and gold brooch, which glittered with every dancing twist she made. And of course, after giving her the brooch, how could Anne refuse to walk to the goods store to buy her grandmother the bottle of the cough syrup that she needed every night?

Anne should have known something bad was going to happen the minute she was in the store. It was dark and cold inside, and Hank was staring without saying a word. There was a strong odor of whisky, and too late, Anne realized that she was the only customer in the darken store, probably already closed for business.

Suddenly conscious of her new stylish look, Anne tried to pull her light shawl to cover as much dress as possible and used a friendly voice as if nothing were unusual. "Oh hi Hank. Grandmother is outside and she asked me to buy her a bottle. You know, the syrup she likes so much."

Hank stared for a long, uncomfortable moment, then looked out to the street, seeing no one through the dusty streaked windows, crowded by shelves filled with goods. Without speaking, Hank pulled a long square bottle filled with dark liquid from a slotted drawer and came out from behind the counter to hand it to Anne. Anne slipped the bottle in her pocket and looked down for just a moment to find the money Grandmother had given her. Then it happened.

It was so fast, yet it seemed to last forever. Hank never said a word. Anne was suddenly on the cold hardwood floor, with a slapping pain from the back of her head to her legs. And then the other pain. Sharp. Tearing. The grunting, muscled, smelly heavy weight ripped and pulled, keeping her pinned to the floor. Then there was laughter.

"I'm so glad you got gussied up for me, An-nee!" Hank snarled. "They'll be toasting me all night at the saloon. But I'll tell'm you're mine now, so don't you worry. No one'll get the idea that you're fancy free."

She could hear the roar of Hank's laughter through the walls and on the street as she ran at full speed up the dirt road, wrapping the loosened and torn fabric close; the fabric that had been so beautiful just minutes earlier. She hadn't stopped running until now.

And by now, every man in Haines had heard what had happened. Hank loved to make trouble, and he loved to brag. And by now, she was sure that the story of Anne's demise included Anne begging and pleading for more, and asking Hank to marry her forever. And by now, someone had gone to the dock from the bar to made sure that Mathew heard that he had lost his girl and to gain favor by buying him a drink. And by now, Mathew knew that Anne had been ruined, for whatever reason. And by now, her life was over. It was time to die.

As she glanced down from looking at the the stars, Anne saw the glitter of a small stream rushing down a mountain to the river. She remembered the stream. It was the one that her family would climb up to and camp overnight at when they walked from Haines to Klukwan, making the travel more of an adventure for the kids. As she looked, she could just make out the jutting large slab of rock that made a perfect large deck, with a view of the merging rivers. Anne regained her feet, which bit with blistering fire. Slowly she made her way up and finally crawled on all fours to reach the large chilled rock, which offered little shelter from the wind.

"This is where I will die," she thought. It made perfect sense to her now. She was ruined. She could not go to heaven. She could never marry Mathew now, not that he would want her now. She couldn't even return to Haines, unless she wanted to work down by the fish docks, hiding during the day from the respectable people. And it would be worse going forward to Klukwan, not that she would be refused. But there would be stares, and silence, and then gentle hints to live with some man or another. It would be too much. She was ruined. Her life was over. Oh, Mathew…

Now, she would not see Elders in heaven. Her only way to enter heaven now was to save someone else's life. That's what the churchman had said, that if you saved a life for God, you went to heaven. Even if you were ruined. But that would not happen. It did not matter. She could not go home. She could not see Mathew.

It was getting cold, and the stars were disappearing in the fast approaching clouds. Anne shivered and thought that she should write a letter. Maybe she could tell Mathew what had happened. But she needed to do it fast before clouds covered all of the moonlight.

Searching for the small pencil she kept in her shawl from the time she attended the little white school as a child, she discovered the square bottle that grandmother was expecting. Anne eyed the dark liquid briefly and opened it. It smelled like grandmother. She remembered the time she had drank some one night after grandmother had fallen asleep. It had made her dizzy and warm, and then sleepy. Anne needed all those feelings now. Quickly she drank the entire contents, and was pleased by the sweet fruity taste that had been warmed by her own heat, held snug to her running body. Putting the bottle back in her pocket, she produced the little stub of a pencil and a scrap of paper that had most of a recipe for the crisp cookies Jill's mother liked to make. Anne had hoped to surprise Mathew with a plate of those cookies for his birthday, only weeks away.

In the wind and fast disappearing moonlight, Anne wrote:

———

Dearest Mathew,

I will love you forever. I am sorry. I do not love THAT MAN.

I love you! I did not want it to happen. I am no good anymore.

You must go on. You must live.

I will be with you forever. Live for both of us.

I love you.
Anne

———

Anne was suddenly dizzy. The rock she was standing on was spinning in large swooping, rocking motions. It scared her as the darkness became thick around her. She had to act quickly. Anne rolled the small letter around her finger making the letter a small scroll and then sealed it in the square bottle. On her knees, she felt and found a crack in the large rock outcropping she was clinging to. She pushed the bottle deep enough to be protected in the rock. To make sure someone who knew her would find the letter, Anne placed the yellow stone and gold brooch her grandmother had given her just above the crack opening. Finally, she placed a tattered strip from the dress she loved so well. "Jill would see that," she thought as the warm softness of passing out into a dreamless sleep flowed over her exhausted body.

* *

Matt did not notice the sunny morning. It was warm and brightly lit for such an early hour as the months of the nightless Alaskan days were fast approaching. Matt ignored the fresh green grass and the rare bright yellow dandelions as he careened his Jeep Cherokee down the winding two-lane bumpy highway, eyes fixated through the cracked windshield. The Chilkat River that bordered the highway for the length of his 30-mile morning commute from Mosquito Lake to Haines was free from ice, but Matt did not notice. He was looking for his tree. The one tree that would end his misery. The tree that would allow him to stop the repeating nightmare of work followed by sleep, with no redeeming reason for being in between.

"Today will be the day," he told himself, and a little smile emerged as he could feel the relief his tree would bring coming closer. Every single horrible day, Matt awoke and started the same old memory in his mind. It was as if a DVD was set on a timer and played in the same order for his amusement, bringing the veil of depression down upon his life before he could drink his first cup of coffee. She was gone. His only love, mother of his children, his wife, Anne. Gone.

"Ann with an E, and not Ann-ee," she would rhyme and did rhyme in his head each morning. She hated it when people added the extra "e" at the end of her name, a fact only he knew and would use in times of argument, which were rare. She countered by reminding him that his name was Mathew, a fact he denied except that Anne controlled possession of the birth certificate that proved it. He loved her so. Beautiful long straight blonde hair accented by the darkest black eyes. Both natural and a rare genetic combination, which led people to believe that one or the other was fake. His body ached for her, he could smell her sweetness at will, but she was gone. It was all gone.

As his drive wore on, the history played out unstoppable in his mind, more real than the road in front of him. The night she went out to a party with her church friends. HER CHURCH FRIENDS, no less. It continued. She didn't come home. The admission of Anne's waking up in bed with Paul. The fight with her pleading that it was not her fault. He wanted to forgive her, but the history played on, uninterrupted, as always: Anne leaving, taking his beautiful daughters away, his drinking, his losing custody to her parents, and finally the telephone call from Anne's parents informing him that Anne had overdosed on Xanax and gin, leaving a note that mentioned him in some manner, and that they were keeping the children with the legal firepower to succeed in doing so.

Matt needed his tree. He had spotted it and worked it out months ago. He had nothing left to offer the last part of his life that had any meaning, his children. Nothing, except the life insurance guaranteed and increased to the maximum that his miserable employer provided, thanks to the heavy-handed union that united all Borough employees. The only trick was that he needed to make sure the event that ended his life was an accident. If he went out and blew his head off with the 12-gauge slug reserved for ornery bears, the coroner's finding of suicide would nullify the insurance payout, and then, even his death would have no point. That's where his tree came in. It was a mammoth cottonwood, a hundred years old and well over a yard across at the base. And very close to the road in the sharp winding area where the wind always blew and the road was always slick. His tree was at about Mile 10, where the rivers came together, and it was nearly ahead. Every day he told himself it would be the day he just swerved a little too sharply, and all his troubles would be ended. Instantly. No more pain, no more depression. No more stupid, boring days, chopping onions and thawing chunks of minced chicken for ungrateful idiots. Just a microsecond of pain and strangeness, as his face moved through the crumbling glass sheet of windshield while his torso ripped into parts, and then, relief. Matt smiled larger. His tree was approaching.

The Jeep rocked as Matt increased his speed and unlatched his seatbelt. He saw the top first, towering over the smaller pines, as he always did. He thought about Anne, and how he might see her soon. Or not. No one really knew. But he did know, his pain was about to end. The tree grew in size rapidly, as Matt rounded the final corner. This was the day! He gripped the steering wheel and held his breath. And then... And then... Nothing. Matt sailed past, the tree shrinking in the rearview mirror. He had chickened out again. He was a loser. Nothing good was waiting for him now for the rest of the day. Just drudgery.

"Oh Anne, I miss you," he muttered. Then the memories started again. As usual.

* *

Anne opened one eye; the other was pinned to the large rock she was lying upon. Her vision was fuzzy and she felt slightly sick to her stomach. The sun was bright and blinding but she was freezing cold. Her legs were painful and numb all at once. She lifted the top part of her body off of the rock with her arms. There was a light coating of snow covering the rocks except where her body had been. She couldn't think clearly. Where was she? Why couldn't she think? Or remember?

Slowly Anne knelt up and finally lifted herself to her feet, with her head and chest hung over, nearly to her knees. Her clothes were in tatters. She had no strength, as if every part of her was bound down with rope or stocking socks. Where was she? Anne tried to straighten up, but was only able to move her head up to the level of her waist. Looking forward, she saw the rocky slope upward, and the new snow, before her muscles gave out and allowed gravity to pull her head down again, arms flinging to her feet.

Gathering her strength for a few moments, Anne rested, and then pulled herself upright, almost to a stand. Her legs started moving, trying to stay under the slow, off-balanced fall that her body was taking sideways. Suddenly, she noticed a sharp pain and strange looseness between her legs as she tried to keep upright. Next was the curious speed with which the trees were passing and the cold chill around her neck as the wind increasingly whipped past her newly shortened hairstyle. And then nothing.

* *

Matt hated his day. What was new? He couldn't take it anymore. It was bad enough that his problem with his drinking had forced him into his eight-dollar-an-hour job, minimum wage for Alaska, even though he held a graduate degree. But did God have to make his boss an illiterate sadist, who's only claim to fame was being the brother-in-law to some big fish muckity-muck in the tiny pond of Haines? Why yell at him about the quality of the no-name discount french-fries that came in 50-pound brown paper sacks, that had been thawed and frozen countless times during their trip on truck beds, ferries, and barges? He had had it. Too much. He began to construct a new plan. A plan that would finally work.

Before starting the 30-mile trip back to Mosquito Lake, Matt stopped at the grocery, liquor, and tackle shop store. "Haven't seen you for a while," the smiling, baseball-capped man said behind the counter, just before returning his gaze to the golf tournament playing out on the television that hung above his head, across from the cigarette selection.

"It's been one of those days," Matt remarked as he hefted the large box containing 5 liters of wine onto the counter.

"I heard that!" as laser light read the box code and presented the purchase price. After an exchange of bills representing the treasure of both the Government of Canada and of the United States, and some quick calculations by the capped man, indicating the experience behind the counter he had acquired, Matt was back in his Jeep, prize in tow. The stale coffee in his traveling mug added a sharp bite to the overly sweet processed wine, but it was cool and refreshing, and it signified a change from moments before, when all was dark.

Matt pulled into the turn-around area along the highway where Tlingit people fished large numbers of salmon for winter during the late summer salmon runs in a tradition known as "subsistence fishing" to Alaskans. It was a special place at that time of year, whereas at other times, it was the closest party spot outside of Haines, where seasonal workers parked their dilapidated school buses for free and burned used pallets to keep mosquitoes at bay. Knowing that the single State Trooper in the Borough had already made his daily trip forty miles to the boarder and back for the day, Matt was safe to drink and then drive back to his home without fear of incarceration. He didn't want to end up in jail again, not now that he had a plan.

As Matt leaned back and relaxed a little, turning the engine off, the memories started, as if some cosmic mind patroller realized that he might be happy just for a second, and needed to bring down the dark curtain of unending misery. There was Anne. He could smell her, he could see her, and he could almost feel her soft warmth. Then the night of the party, the fight, the loss of his children... As he followed through the memories and pivoted to his plan and his awaiting tree, his plan at once unraveled, snapping his body forward. It suddenly occurred to him that if he drank wine and crashed into his tree, the insurance company would use that as an excuse not to pay his kids. They would try any excuse not to pay, and drinking and driving was probably somewhere in the fine print.

He started the engine quickly and threw the just opened treasure of wine out of the window. Some underpaid shift worker would undoubtedly consider this a good day when they found it. He had only taken a few sips and if he hurried, it wouldn't be in his bloodstream yet enough to be considered impairing, if any part of him remained. Matt kept his gas tank and bumper gas cans filled to their limits in hopes of improving his odds for success. A different level of excitement quickly consumed him. This WAS the day he finally would crash into his tree.

From the direction he was traveling from Haines, he could see his tree for a greater time. Sweat dripped from his forehead, further indicating that this was truly the day. He had only moments left to live, as his tree grew in size. What should he think about? His mind was blank. And then Anne. As bright, and shinning, and loving, as the time they were most in love. Right in front of him, as if she were part of the cracked windshield that allowed the silhouette of the great tree to merge with her face somehow.

And then…And then…He swung the wheel and the Jeep plunged straight at the trunk. Matt experienced no microsecond of pain as he had always anticipated, just a sensation of lifting from his seat and bumping his head on the roof. Then nothing.

* *

Anne's body fed five ravens, three eagles, and a small family of wolves that kept to themselves rather than running in the local pack. All would have had difficulty making it through the unusually cold winter if it had not been for her. But Anne was not there. She was gone. She felt nothing.

* *

Matt awoke in his Jeep. He could tell where he was because his head was on the passenger side floor mat and his torso was straddling the emergency brake, a position he had awaken to before during his drinking days. He hadn't been out long because the sun had only shifted slightly in position in the sky from when he had started out from town. He had blown it again. Pushing hard on the bent door to get out, Matt realized the problem with his new strategy. Approaching from the town side, there was a hidden ditch in the grass before his tree. It occurred to him that he had not really studied the situation as well as he imagined each morning. The Jeep was bent beyond running however; at least he had accomplished that. Rolling himself backwards, he screamed at the sky, and then the mountains.

He had had it. Matt became resolute. He had come too close. He had to just suck it up, be a man, and get it over with. Enough with elaborate plans. Looking at the rushing silt-filled river, he considered drowning himself. But that seemed too chancy. He'd probably just get cold and end up racking up a bill at the medical clinic for warm I.V.s and warm enemas. Then Matt looked in the other direction and saw the answer. A small stream rushed off the mountain with a large rock ledge jutting out from the mountain about a third of the way up.

Without thinking he rushed over and up. Matt scrambled up the sliding loose slate, grabbing trees and shrubs keep balance. He followed the little stream, practically crawling at times until he reached the ledge. Shaking the dust from his pants and wiping the blood from his bleeding palms caused by the sharp stone, Matt surveyed the valley and the rivers that merged below in front of his eyes. The rock was large and flat, about the size of his deck at home, with a few large cracks about.

"This is it. This is where my life ends. My life is over," he told himself with conviction.

Slowly he inched to the edge and peered down. Yes, it would work. There were many jagged chunks of slate below and the drop was clear and long. Matt backed up and felt the excitement again. It was about to be over. The pain would end. But he hesitated, just a second, when the glint of a yellow gemstone caught his eye. He lowered his head and saw the gold and stone brooch and retrieved it. Suddenly forgetting his mission, he examined the clasp and makers mark, and began to reflect on the hours of watching "Antiques Roadshow" with Anne. It was old, and perhaps worth something. Now curious, he reached into the crack further and retrieved the square bottle, sealed with a slip of paper inside. A new thrill rattled through Matt. It was a treasure map, or something equally fun and exciting, he was sure. All thought of jumping off of the ledge momentarily left him. He carefully opened the bottle and unraveled the yellowed, old letter. It was written to HIM. He fell back as he read the words written decades earlier:

———

Dearest Mathew,

I will love you forever. I am sorry. I do not love THAT MAN.

I love you! I did not want it to happen. I am no good anymore.

You must go on. You must live.

I will be with you forever. Live for both of us.

I love you.

Anne

———

Matt never again thought about ending his life. After spending the rest of the evening into night sitting on the rock ledge reading and re-reading the letter, he decided that there was some amount of divine magic involved, or some astronomically high odds at play for events to occur as they had. It didn't really matter which was the truth; he had no choice but to accept the reality of the event and to live as human testimony, proof of the impossible nature of the universe. He was cured. He loved Anne as much as ever. And he would live for both of them. A good life, he promised himself, and her. And it was.

* *

Anne was suddenly awake. It had been a long time since she had been awake, she realized. There had been a long, dreamless, dark period, from which, it had been judged somehow, that she was never to return from. But now, Anne felt wonderful. She remembered everything, all at once; from birth to the moment she fell against the hard stone in her new hairstyle. And the memories were glorious, not painful at all. There was light, and lightness. Someone was holding her hand. She knew that person's name was Anne also, "…with an E, and not Ann-ee…" she heard in her mind as the woman smiled.

"Thank you," said Anne with an E, and not Ann-ee. And Anne became not ruined, and cried with joy as Mathew grabbed her and kissed her long. Forever.

IT HAPPENED ALONG THE HAINES

HAVEN HAINES

T he bank robbery had not gone well. Tom had told his brother that a quick stick-up of a large grocery store would have netted the pair the same amount of money without causing a media stir. But Ed wouldn't listen. "One big heist and back to the beaches of L.A.," was Ed's mantra. Tom came to believe that Ed wanted publicity in order to have a good story to tell around the campfire while the next generation of surfer-wannabes proved their reverence. Tom did not share Ed's goal nor did he have any real love of California. His secret hopes included a life of simple living in a small town in the woods, one free from any unusual attention. Desired or not, Ed's publicity was now historical fact, an amount of fame that would follow him into the Canadian legal system and determine the outcome of his remaining pointless life. Tom was on his own.

In truth, Ed's plan for the bank was perfectly conceived. In and out in less than five minutes with not a single shot fired. If only Ed had been able to control his nervousness, he might not have struck the bank manager with his gun, breaking her jaw. As the Fates had designed, with their continual provision of bad luck for Tom and Ed, the bank manager turned out to be the wife of one of the highest-ranking public officials in Edmonton, *Lord Snoot* or something like that, who was regarded quite highly. To further complicate matters, at the time of the heist, a home video was filmed from across the street by a Provincial tourist who had been awed by the modern cement structures, capturing the clear image of Ed and Tom, as well as the red Honda used for the escape. The astronomical odds of such coincidental bad luck furthered Tom's theory that there existed a divine conspiracy that ensured that the brothers would be deprived from enjoying their time on Earth.

After the unintentionally aggravated robbery, the two brothers had split the pile of brightly colored bills and made their plan. Ed took the Honda, which he planned to ditch in Calgary before catching a bus, while Tom took the Jeep with the California license plates registered in his name. Both were to make their way back to the Oceanview Motel alone and meet up on the beach. By the time Tom had stopped to buy gas for the journey home, he saw the image of Ed being drug along in handcuffs by two sharply-dresses Mounties on the small television behind the cashier's counter of the convenient store at which he had stopped. Ducking into the bathroom, Tom managed to cut his hair into a crooked flattop style and remove his moustache with the little two-inch scissors mounted to his Swiss army knife. Tom convinced himself that his new disguise was successful, as the cashier who had just been staring at his grainy portrait provided in the breaking news newscast failed to recognize him.

Realizing his new status as a wanted man, Tom had decided to head north. He knew that the plan between the brothers included the contingency of not talking to the authorities if either were caught. But Tom also knew it would take no time for cops to figure out that Ed was from California, that he was Ed's brother, and that in all likelihood he would attempt to get out of Canada. Going north was the only hope for outsmarting the authorities. Now, with nearly an entire day of driving behind him and with a deep mind-clogging haze that results from two days without sleep making it hard to remember the logical arguments for his actions plaguing him, Tom pulled the hot and dusty Jeep into a parking area with two outhouses and a sign describing the historical value of the rough-hewn log bridge in the distance. Within 10 seconds he was asleep.

With a jolt, Tom awakened. The Jeep was very hot with the brightness of midday making it difficult to focus. Tom jumped. A second series of loud raps on the driver's side window made Tom realize what had awoken him. Rolling down the window, Tom stared without talking at the large man with a badge representing some branch of the Canadian authority system that he did not recognize.

"Good day! Sir, I need to ask you to move your vehicle to one side as the manner in which you parked creates navigational problems for the people with families needing to use the facilities."

Tom froze, suddenly awake, but unable to speak. The robbery, the image of his brother being arrested, and his own image on the television flooded his mind. A quick glance to the side revealed that not only was the bag that contained the pounds of stolen bills and loonys in plain site, but also the butt of the revolver used in the robbery from underneath the bag. Before he could move, the man continued.

"Do you speak English?" the uniformed man said slowly.

"Oh, oh, I'm sorry officer," Tom forced out with the tail end of a deep breath, deciding to take a chance. "I was sleeping, as you saw. I'm on vacation from the States. I didn't realize how far it was between motels up here...I was so tired. I don't want to cause any trouble."

"No trouble, but I advise you to realign your vehicle according to the prescribed design. Yes, the Yukon is a little sparse. You're not in Kansas anymore." Tom began sweating. Was that a joke? Should he laugh? Was he being toyed with? He saw that he was indeed in the middle of a parking area taking up three parking spots. Several older people dressed in polyester were climbing in and out of RVs parked at improvised odd angles, all staring at him.

"Heh-heh. You sure are right about that. Can you tell me how far the next town is so that I might rest, *in proper fashion*?" Tom attempted to match the formal speech of the badge-wearing man.

As the officer turned, pointed up the highway, and gave directions, Tom quickly shifted the bag in the seat next to him to cover the gun, "Haines Junction is only a few kilometers ahead. You will find several clean establishments that will provide lodging for the night." Tom thanked the man and tried not to appear anxious as he pulled out of roadside attraction into the traffic of the Yukon portion of the Alaskan Highway. The officer followed directly behind for several miles. Tom could see that he was talking to someone on his police radio. This would be the end. Undoubtedly the call letters of his license plate had set off every alarm in the local police station as the dispatcher typed them into the computer. Surely, he thought, the officer was simply following to prevent Tom from backing out of roadblock trap which now lay ahead. His chest began to hurt. Tom decided that he should turn himself in without a fight when stopped as he felt as though he were about to pass out at any moment.

Just as his Jeep pulled into the five or six blocks along the highway that represented the town of Haines Junction, the officer turned around and headed back in the direction they had both traveled. Tom slowed into the Shell station, turned off the engine, and shook. Slowly, the sweat stopped pouring from his brow and the sharp ache in his chest eased. He needed to get out of this country and hole up somewhere before he ended up in a hospital from a heart attack. Washing up in the men's room, he bought a new tee shirt and a few bottles of iced tea before paying for the items and the tankful of gas he had pumped with some of the brightly colored Canadian bills that had ruined his life to obtain. He was grateful to see that the attendant was watching an action show in a Chinese language on the store's television and not a local news channel.

"What is the quickest route to America from here?" Tom asked.

With a bit of a scowl the man replied, "Well, if you mean Alaska, both of these roads will take you there," pointing out of the window. "You do know that Canada is part of North America don't you?"

"I'm sorry, I'm just a bit lost," Tom said, feeling a tightness return to his chest, realizing that had again drawn attention to himself.

"If you go straight, it's about 200 kilometers to the Alaskan boarder outside of Haines. If you turn up, you'll be in Alaska in about twice that."

Thanking the man, and exiting quickly before being recognized, Tom changed his shirt and followed the sign that pointed to Haines. He never tried to calculate kilometers, but he knew he had to get back to his country, *America*, as quickly as possible. Cops in America wouldn't be looking for a two-bit crook from a different country. They have enough to worry about in their own country. Haines. If he could make it, it would be his haven. No need to get to California now that Ed was locked up. Haven Haines. A few short kilometers, whatever distance that was, and he'd be safe.

The soothing colors of the grasses on the rolling hills, the lack of traffic, and the cool iced tea helped bring about a calming Tom had not felt for days. He began to daydream when he remembered just how close he had come to being caught only an hour before. Tom stopped his Jeep beside a large lake and removed his gun. It was warm and heavy. He had hated it from the first. With its short barrel and line marks scratched onto the plastic handle, it had obviously been used for the only purpose it had, to shoot at people. The hardened street peddler who sold it to Ed for only $100 must have known it was used in some unscrupulous and traceable act. Tom agreed to hold it in the robbery, but had vowed to himself not to pull the trigger, no matter what. Tom mused to himself about how the gun skipped like a flat rock on the lake water when he tossed it and how he and Ed would skip rocks for hours on Shaver Lake in California as kids. Tom also wondered what other crimes Ed had been connected with from the gun he had undoubtedly been caught with, as Ed loved guns and would never have parted with his willingly.

Tom suddenly realized that although he was in the most remote area of the world that he had ever been, there might still be people watching him. Only a criminal would want to throw a gun in a lake. What if he had been seen? And what if the gas attendant had recognized him after he left? Or the officer after he had returned to his station? What if the money he had used was traceable with some invisible ink? He had to hurry. Tom's chest began to hurt again.

Pushing the Jeep to 70-miles-an-hour, Tom traveled over a summit and then down in elevation to the border. Only after seeing a fully-grown bear with a cub did he slow his speed down a bit. Hitting something that large at full speed would be worse than ending up in jail. As he approached the border, he decided to just leave the money in the bag and put it in the back. All or nothing he figured. If the Jeep were searched, they would find the money anyway, so better not to hide it. He could always claim that he won the lottery or something. At that thought, Tom laughed out loud. Even his laugh was shaky. His chest began to hurt again but it was too late to change course. The speed signs ordered him to a crawl as he passed the Canadian customs to the left. After what seemed like miles in slow motion, Tom was suddenly in front of what looked like a tollbooth with several customs agents all looking at him.

The men made Tom wait for what felt like ten minutes before one approached. Without smiling, the guard started in, trying to trip him up. Tom answered as he had been practicing for the last hour. "I'm on vacation...I've always wanted to see Haines...from California...I bought a tee shirt and some food." Tom handed him his driver's license and passport. The guard walked back to the booth. Obviously, he had been unimpressed with his answers. The pain in his chest was unbearable. It was all over, and all of the faces connected to the uniforms behind the bulletproof glass knew it. As soon as the computer connected his license with his crime the guns would be coming out. As he saw it, there were only two choices, either he could gun his Jeep as fast a possible, dodge the bullets, and go as deep into the woods as possible, which were undoubtedly as charted and familiar to the local patrolmen as the L.A. beaches were to Tom, or to just give up before getting shot.

The armed men sent the first guard back to the Jeep. Just before Tom could surrender, the customs official asked, "You're going to Haines?" Tom held his breath and nodded. "Then you want to stay on this road. *Don't get off of this road* until you get to town." With that order, the man handed the driver's license and passport back.

Tom was paralyzed. Should he confess now? His heart pounded. The customs agent stared at him then finally made a gesture to move ahead. Then, as if commanded magically by the hand wave, his body slowly eased the Jeep forward and he was again driving down the highway. But before his mind could recover or his heart could stop aching, the rear view mirror reflected the fact that a dark sedan with another officer driving it had pulled out behind Tom and had begun to follow him, matching his exact speed. He had been allowed to pass through the border, but only to make sure that he arrived somewhere where an arrest could be exploited, Tom thought. When he got to Haines, they would probably just open fired on him. That way the locals would all become heroes and the town would get the glory instead of the customs people.

A rat trapped in a cage, Tom thought. The miles slowly ticked away. Tom reached in back and pulled the bag with all the bright bills to the front seat. He gazed at all the Canadian "monopoly" money as he drove, just so that he would be able to fully remember it when he spent the rest of his life in jail. He could have lived for years on the stash and had some great parties, he thought. He was tempted to lift it up so that the following officer could have a good gaze too as he pursued at 55-miles-an-hour, but decided against it. The life he had always wanted was so close. He could have just bought one of the little log cabins that now occasionally dotted the riverside of the silt-filled river the highway followed and lived there quietly for the rest of his life. But obviously, that dream would not happen now. Then, without warning, a restaurant appeared, indicated by the sign that read "33 Mile Roadhouse," with 33 miles yet to go to get to the town of Haines. Being open, it beckoned to provide Tom with his last meal. Parking, he looked up to see if his escort had stopped. But instead of stopping, the dark car continued without wavering until out of sight.

Ordering the largest hamburger to go, Tom paid with a fresh Canadian $100 bill. The young lady began to make a bit of a fuss about making change until Tom told her to keep the change. He was celebrating his new hope that perhaps he had made it free after all. But his hopes were immediately dashed. "You sure look familiar," the lady started. "Are you on television? It seems like I know you. Were you on 'Gold Rush'?" Seeing the television in the corner of the dining area and that it was tuned to a news program, Tom thanked the woman, took his meal, and hastily made his way back on the highway to Haines.

Tom's mind raced and his heart pounded. There was no one in the mirror. But if every waitress recognized his face, then the news media must have it plastered everywhere. He was doomed to be caught. Or was he just being paranoid? He was in America. It was Alaska, but still America. Why would they care about crimes committed in Canada? He had to relax. Just get to Haines. Haven Haines.

This last bit of road had spectacular views. High mountains next to a meandering river provided a naturally soothing reaction in Tom. After driving for a thousand miles, the Jeep almost drove itself, allowing him to think. As a car came towards him in the opposite direction and passed, the driver motioned to him. Panic struck. Why would someone make a gesture to him? It's not like anyone in Alaska would know him...*or would they*! His heart pounded again. Did the driver wave or was he warning Tom?

Tom kept driving. He must be going nuts. His mind was out of control. Just keep driving, he told himself. He passed another car. Nothing. See, you are just imagining things. Then a truck came around a bend and passed. This time an elderly man lifted his whole arm to gesture as he passed. Tom heard himself yelp, which startled him even more, as he heard his own inhuman sound reverberate about the inside of the windshield.

"I did not imagine that," Tom told himself aloud. "That was real." His chest hurt sharply, as if one of his ribs were broken. First the customs guard ordered me to stay on the road into Haines and now everyone recognizes me, he thought. There must be a posse waiting, they probably still do that in Alaska. Just then, an airplane came in close behind him and buzzed its engine loudly as it appeared to land between the river and the road. "They must have been watching me from the air too!"

The last bit of sanity grabbed Tom's mind. You are over-reacting, it sounded. Yes, maybe it is just coincidence. Then he passed the sign, which showed that there actually was an airport beside the road. Yes, just coincidence that the only plane spy plane in Alaska landed just as he came to town. The sweat dripped from his forehead, burning as it fell into his eye. As he wiped his eye while driving past a house with a garden, an older man laughed as he waved to Tom, causing him to swerve the Jeep.

Tom screamed. He gunned the accelerator as fast as it would go. Tom yelled as he rounded the corner, not seeing the signs that lowered the speed limit to 35 MPH. Within an instant, he had turned a corner coming face to face with the totem pole edged sign welcoming Tom to the city of Haines, his haven. Standing on his brake pedal, the Jeep slid sideways stopping short of causing damage to older log buildings behind the sign. As the Fates had planned, and as predicted by Tom, a large SUV adorned with red lights with a Haines police officer inside had been stopped at that moment at a stop sign on a road that intersected the highway at the entryway to the town. Tom jumped from the Jeep with his bag of bills and coins and ran into a nearby RV park, screaming wildly at the vacationing inhabitants to leave him alone. Within moments, Tom was handcuffed, read his rights, confessed to robbing a bank, and was led to the SUV for the ride down the last bit of the highway to the police station.

As the police-equipped SUV made its way, Tom questioned the officer, "How did you do it? I'm a thousand miles from Edmonton. How did you get everyone to recognize me?"

"I don't understand," stated the officer dryly.

"They all knew me. The waitress, the people passing by, the old man in the garden. They all knew me and signaled me and laughed and smiled. How did you know

I was coming? And how did you alert them all to recognize me? Why didn't you shoot me?"

The officer shifted, wondering if he should continue. "Well, I realize you are from California, and I know that things are different down there. But around here, people just tend to wave when you pass by. People are just friendly I guess." Then, as if cued, a young lady walking by the side of the road waved to the officer as the SUV passed. "And as far as shooting, Alaskans probably have a different approach. Unless you are an ornery bear, we tend to ask first and shoot later."

"Y-you mean, you wouldn't have caught me if I hadn't have sped into town and crashed?" Tom chest pain returned worse than ever.

"Nope. You would have been accepted as one of the town. With all the money you had with you, you could have lived here for years in luxury. It would have been the perfect haven. Haven Haines, you could say."

Tom yelled, then slumped over, turning blue in color. The officer sped directly to the medical clinic two blocks away. Within a minute, CPR was initiated by a team that consisted of one doctor and several nurses, all working hard to save Tom's life. The rescue efforts proved futile, although heroically continued for half-an-hour. Tom was dead.

Upon the return of the stolen money, the Government of Canada decided that they had no use for the body Tom. Some in the Borough of Haines, feeling that they had played a part in the demise of Tom, created a silent fund, which allowed a resting place in the back end of the local cemetery. Many years later, an older and humbler Ed passed through the town of Haines.

In jail, Ed had been told that his brother had been seen in Haines, but there was no trial and there was no record of the arrest as far as he could piece together. One of the things that had kept him alive while in prison was Ed's belief that the robbery had been worth it and that Tom had been living the quiet life in a small town that he had always talked of. But Ed's hope of reuniting for one last adventure ended the day he found a small plaque in the back of the little Haines cemetery. The plate read:

Here lies Tom

He found a haven in Haines

"Good for you, brother," Ed told the ground that held Tom's remains. With that, Ed took his leave, filled with inspiration, and spent remainder of his law-abiding life assisting others in benevolent programs that provided assistance to people living in small towns.

DAWN ALONG THE HAINES HIGHWAY

I t had been a long time, perhaps a decade, since Craig had awoken with a hangover of this magnitude. He had been making his moonshine religiously from part of the yearly raspberry crop and from the rare find of an intact bag of sugar or can of sweetened fruit for as long as could remember. But such finds had become almost an impossible memory now, and every drop of precious homemade alcohol was needed to complete his medical emergency kit, the last holdover from one of his previous occupations as a hospital nurse. Rolling over, he became breathless at the sight, and seeing the naked young woman sleeping next to him trustingly, with a light smile on her face, he remembered why he had emptied the delicious antiseptic from the bottle the night before. He had made his decision.

Stroking her light brown strands, completely untangled now, Craig closed his eyes and let the pulsing throb punctuate the recall of recent memories. It had taken so long to gain the feral child's trust. The first time he had "met" her, he was not sure she was a human. In fact, he had been certain that she was a bear and that he had fooled himself that he had seen something that he knew could not be real for the hundredth time. Craig thought about that that day and the long walk out of the woods, from the house he had lived in and loved since the time of money, to the last remnants of the Haines Highway. Once, the highway was the only two lanes of asphalt from the Pacific Ocean in Haines, Alaska, a town of 1,500 people at one time, to the town of Haines Junction in the Yukon of Canada with 500 people, over a hundred miles away. Once, he had tried to walk up the road to Canada only to give up and return due to the washed out bridges, buried sections, and complete absence of any building or supplies along the broken path. Plus, there was the fact that he was so old, something that he absolutely needed to deny if he were to enjoy his time as the last man on Earth.

The section of the highway Craig traveled that day he met her was well known to him, as it was the only passageway to the headwaters of the Chilkat River that paralleled it. One could be forgiven for not recognizing it as the reliable thoroughfare it had once been, with the sapling trees that had grown right through the asphalt and the grasses that rose through the cracking and uneven surface. The highway now reminded Craig more of a Roman cobblestone path than of the lifeline of resources and American culture it had once been. But even in the unrecognizable and decrepit state, the highway represented the greatest example of the mighty infrastructure still remaining in his world that once required large governments to create. It was the last evidence that he had once been a great master over nature, with great powers at his disposal, including the ability to move up and down the path at high speed and for any desired distance with virtually no physical effort. He missed his Jeep.

Craig had been pushing through the growth on the highway to try his luck at stabbing fish with his three-pronged walking stick at the spot across from Porcupine Creek where the gray-colored glacier silt filled river spread out to run a quarter-mile wide and three inches deep. There had been a period over a decade long when Craig thought he would never again see another fish. Maybe it had been the Disease, or the radiation, or some other toxin, he never would know. But lately, fish had been returning to the rivers. Life had become much easier in Craig's "retirement" after age 65 when it only took a walk to the river to secure a fine meal of salmon or other species that had taken to the clean but silt-filled freshwater. He remembered the moment, when out of the corner of his eye, he saw the movement of shadows. That movement always demanded reaction in the woods. Usually, movement was related to a startled bird, but occasionally it meant that there was a crossing of paths with a bear or moose where one's life was on the line. This one time, the movement was instantly recognized and memorized. It appeared to be the bare backside of a young woman running away. But did the one-second observation really occur? Obviously not, he had reasoned. He had not seen another human since the summer of the Disease. He knew it must have been a trick of light and shadow improperly registered by his old, tired eyes. It had most likely been a bear he had decided. But the one-second of image had been deeply and permanently burned into the memory center in his forgetful brain. Even now, lying next to the beautiful nature-child, he could see every detail of that instant in his mind, and he fully realized the magnitude of that chance encounter. Out of all the billions of seconds of information his brain had recorded from his eyes, it was humbling to understand that one divine instant of memory can change everything in one's life, and perhaps change everything for an entire planet.

Craig could have ignored what he had seen, and almost did. It was not until two days later, with the one-second memory having been replayed hundreds of times in his mind, that he retraced his steps and found the thin footpath hidden by brush in the gully that served as the drainage way for the highway. A mix of excitement, fear, and anger fueled him for days, practically without food or sleep, as he combed the woods for other signs of human activity. He had looked for years for signs of life, digging through houses, leaving behind signs with directions to his house, listening for short wave transmissions, and traveling as far as the highway would allow passage. The only hope he was ever afforded was the sight of the remaining artificial satellites that moved with their unnatural speed across the night starscape. Craig surprised himself at the amount of anger the idea of another human living right in his midst generated. How many years of loneliness could have been avoided? Was he not the last living human? Must he now be responsible for future generations again? The only solace he was able to derive from his life up to that point that saved him from his severe bouts of depression was the understanding that he was the last human, and that the planet could finally heal itself after he took the last meddling member of his species to the grave with him when he died. Ever since he could remember, Craig truly hated humans, in general. To Craig, it appeared to him that humans always chose the path of war, fighting, and destruction, even when they knew what was right course of action. Humans were always greedy, and lied at every turn to make excuses. He hated people, as a mischievous mob, at a distance. He had always worked to keep people at a distance. But Craig was also lonely, a pain he also hated, and missed the occasional personal contact that he could tolerate. The thought that he was not the last human after all stirred anew his burning anger that gave his tired body the energy to continue his search in the woods.

Her home was indicated by the freshly downed grass pathway leading to a small cabin Craig did not know existed in a mostly cottonwood forest that had no turnoff from the highway. The people who had lived there in the time of money must have parked on the highway and used snowmachines to access their home. The area around the gray, aged-wood structure with a green metal roof was littered with broken glass vessels, split food cans, and scraps of various plastic and cardboard containers. Inside, the main room was filled from wall to wall with clothes, rugs, blankets, and furs of every kind. The aroma of rot and mold was overwhelming, but the sight of recent human activity excited Craig to the point that he could barely move about due to his shaking hands and legs. In one corner, great collections of dried berries and whole dried fish were found in stacks of bowls and vessels, covered with old, stained plastic scraps. The door and windows were covered and bound with layers of clothing leaving the cabin dark but deliberately airtight. It was apparent that countless hours of human desperation had been expended in the hope of keeping the below zero Alaskan winter out of this one room, cloth-filled refuge. A small opening in the fabric-layered webs led to what had been the kitchen area and the only other room in the home. Scattered light from a dirt-covered window still framed by bright yellow drapes allowed Craig to make out the morbid vision that he had witnessed a hundred times before but had never become nonchalant about. Two clothed skeletons, in positions as if posed for a haunted house ride in an amusement park, remained on guard, claiming their right of ownership to the dark and empty kitchen that had once been the heart of a family. Without considering the remains of the couple, the kitchen appeared intact and normal to the time of money, and mostly unchanged by the passage of time. Dishes and towels were in place; even the soap remained on the sink corner. Odd that the room had not been incorporated into the rest of the small cabin area, Craig thought. The room had been deliberately kept as a crypt, not changed since the time of the Disease, but not sealed either. It was obvious that the family that owned the cabin was still together, with the only difference in the dynamic from the other scores of homes Craig had raided over the past uncounted years being that one member of this clan was apparently still walking around.

And now, she was in his bed. "You sure were a hard catch," Craig said aloud. She stirred slightly, smiling in her half-asleep state, and moving her body until the warm nakedness melted with his skin. Craig almost recoiled from the feeling before curling his body to touch her more. He had been alone for so long that the feeling of a living thing touching him triggered a subconscious warning that directed him to flee. It would take a while to unlearn that reaction, he thought. Craig wondered what she thought he had just said to her. It didn't really matter what he said, her reaction in return was generally one of affection, similar to a pet cat, just happy to know that he was around to feed her and pet her. It was also something more, of course. Craig was the end of her long loneliness, as she was his. What luck that she was such a beauty, and one who was not used to wearing clothes, he mused. If it were still the time of money, he would have been scorned for even approaching a woman of her age and body.

Craig's head ached. He obviously had really become a lightweight in recent years. There was a time when he could finish off several bottles of wine and shake it off in the morning with a couple cups of coffee. There was something about having a headache that he thought he should remember for an instant. But not being able to immediately recall it, he closed is eyes and relived the memory of the long process it took to finally bring her back to his home.

After Craig had discovered her home, which irritated him no end, being that he had been living within a few miles of her without any idea that she had been there all those years, he embarked on a summer-long effort of attracting her to his side. At first, he lived at the site, although he was unable to palate the smell of the cabin. He generally slept outdoors, fashioning a campfire and stove from camping equipment he found unused in a shed. He could have alleviated years of suffering from her life if he had only located her earlier and enlightened her to the power of fire. It was hard for him to believe that she had not smelled his fires over the years. Perhaps she had known that he had been living in her area all of her life. Maybe, Craig hoped, she would learn to talk and tell him her life story before he died from old age.

After weeks of yelling into the woods for her to come back to her home, Craig spent countless days hunting the local woods for signs. He systematically combed the riverside, all the standing homes in the area, and the berry patches for signs of the human he only knew from the one-second vision burned in his brain. Craig even ventured into the Native Alaskan village of Klukwan, thinking that it might be her second home where she could hide because he rarely visited it. He loved the Tlingit culture as it was portrayed in history books. Having attended the University of Alaska, he had spent considerable time studying totem poles and carvings created by Native masters, and learned as much basic Tlingit language as he could easily remember without frustration. Try as he might, he could never get the deep throat sounds and abrupt stops to sound correct. But the Disease had taken all the Tlingit people he knew along with everyone else and had emptied the village that once promised wonderment and exotic language. Craig always felt apprehensive being in the silent little town as if thousands of years of ancestors were watching his activities of looting unused supplies. In the scattered newer cabins and homes in the Borough made by non-Natives, he only felt as if the present skeletons had reason to watch him from beyond death. He had learned to counter the feeling by talking to the dead homeowners, some of which he knew in the time of money, and thanking them for their leftovers from life. Craig searched through the village town, stopping to marvel anew at some of the few ancient Tlingit art pieces still hidden in the slowly crumbling structures. He understood that they were priceless items, never to be replicated, and again he desired to take some back to his home to revere and keep safe for the future. Taking anything but food from the town would have crossed some cultural boundary he figured, somehow, in some way that made no sense now that everyone was dead. Still, the need to respect the boundary commanded him. Scouring the dirt pathways he heard no sounds and saw no footprints or other new clues. Craig decided that he must have scared her off from the area entirely, perhaps never to return. In desperation and despair, he returned to her aged cabin to see if there had been any hints he had missed.

It was almost comical, Craig thought in retrospect. He had bumbled around the entire stretch of the highway for the better part of a month thinking that he was the great and educated hunter easily stalking his prey. Since that time, having spent time with her and witnessing her innate abilities to slide silently through brush that he could only navigate with loud thrashing using a machete, and her ability to disappear from sight in the shallowest of forest shadows at any moment, he realized now that she may have been following him the entire time, perhaps even wanting to be found out, but not knowing his motives she would have been cautious. He had tried hiding in her cabin noiselessly for days. He tried smoking volumes of fish and squirrel, an activity that ended in only attracting a member of a local bruin family. He tried putting clear jars of berries in spots of cleared brush, where sunlight brightly lit the collected treasures. Nothing had worked. Craig had almost resigned himself to the despair that he would spend another winter aging alone.

In the end, the magical day when Craig became part of a couple, and the human race had a chance to repopulate the clean slate of a planet, the moment of contact happened without apparent reason or through coaxing by him at all. Craig was sitting in front of the old cabin, mostly concentrating on the intricacies associated with stoking the campfire for maximum burn time for the evening, when she simply appeared silently from the woods, walked to the fire, and crouched down at the opposite side of the flames from him. She cooed lightly as she moved her mostly naked torso side to side to feel the warmth. Any movement or sound made that night by Craig sent her jumping back from the fire several feet, at times making her turn as if about to run away. But she never did leave, and never left his side from the first.

In the days that followed, she became accustomed to Craig's movements and eventually lost the instinct to flee. She obsessed over his every movement, appearing to mimic, or try to mimic, every action Craig made. Her first study was of fire, in which she learned the pain of burns, the need for feeding fire with wood, the use of smoke in moving mosquitoes back, and the joy of cooked meat and heated teas. All activity and learning occurred at a distance at that time. She always kept at least a yard or two apart from him and items had to be left rather than passed between them. Every attempt Craig made to touch her ended in a period of uneasiness in which the customary distance between them increased for an interval directly proportional to the overt nature of the attempt.

And now, she was in his bed. Opening his eyes, and squinting in the bight sunlight that had begun to stream into the bedroom, Craig stroked his hands down her naked body, pulling her buttocks to his groin under the sheets and allowed the ancient impulse of pleasure begin to stimulate and warm his tired body. He at once lost his desire to seek a glass of water to help deaden his throbbing head, the only cure to counter the dehydration at the heart of a hangover. It seemed as if a lifetime had passed since the first time he had felt her skin next to his, and now he wondered if he could ever live without her warm body within reach. But was it love? He enjoyed the physical pleasure. But he had never loved anyone, as far as he could tell. People were the enemy. He wondered if he might experience that mystic feeling this time, with her.

The first time he held her they were still at her old cabin, the day they left it for the ages to live in his modern Alaskan home in the town of Mosquito Lake. Mosquito Lake had been an unincorporated town of about 120 people who lived in cabins and houses along a three-mile stretch of road that was paved between the Haines Highway and the natural little lake in the woods where swans sometimes lived. After the Disease, the road and the homes became Craig's entire universe, with all of the portable riches from the three-mile road having long been transported to his house via wheelbarrow or motorcycle. After he made contact with her, the lifestyle of camping at her cabin without the amenities Craig had grown accustom to had begun to wear thin. His home was equipped with plumbing fed by a tapped spring, wood stoves for heating and cooking, televisions and DVD players plugged into an electrical supply generated by both wind and running water, stores of food from the time of money, and most importantly, soaps and deodorants. He knew that as the fire had been the source of endless wonderment in her new life, the treasures of the retained modern lifestyle from the time of money at his home would become a virtual amusement park of pleasure and excitement. Before leaving her cabin, Craig entered to search for any items he believed she might wish to take with her, with her following him inside, two paces back and with the door propped open. The smell instantly decided for Craig that she would be acquiring a new wardrobe at his home. The only non-cloth items about included sticks that had been used for some unknown purpose and the stacks of bowls with foodstuff dried within them. The food and cloth should stay, Craig determined, as the cabin would serve as a safehouse if ever either of them found themselves in need while in the area. Besides, he considered, maybe she would need the home to return to if their new relationship didn't hold. He had never been able to keep a relationship going before, due to his general dislike of others. He moved to enter the kitchen area where the skeletonized remains of her family still kept watch when their first skin-to-skin contact was made. She leaped at Craig, jumped on his back, and pulled him to the floor. He had been paralyzed and began to stammer as the cascade from the astonishing observation flooded his brain. First, the young woman had a formidable strength. She had instantly floored him and successfully dragged him relentlessly from the doorway opening despite his attempts to stand up and regain composure. Second, she vocalized for the first time a series of sounds that could only be considered some personal language that had an intent or meaning behind them. Craig immediately translated her commands as, "You stay out of there!" It struck him at that moment for the first time that she had the ability to speak and that it would only be a matter of time before he would teach her to communicate her thoughts in English. But the rush of joy that the thought of communication had brought to him at that moment was superceded at once, and forever, by an entirely animalistic wave of pleasure, warmth, and ecstasy that enraptured both of them into an hour long trance. Craig allowed himself to become one with her in an embrace, in a manner he could not remember ever attempting before, on a pile of moldy blankets and towels, in the dark, unheated cabin to which they would never return, while she explored every part of Craig's body with her dirty but surprisingly soft fingers.

Craig became physically excited remembering her first embrace of him, and she was now awake, rubbing her naked body against his. Even at his advanced age, he was not sure he could resist her. She would become wild at times like this when they were together, rubbing herself hard against him, and apparently not quite sure what she wanted from him for pleasure. Craig had been able to track her menstrual cycle since their meeting three months earlier and knew that it would be at about this time that ovulation would occur. He could only wonder if such times of the menstrual cycle truly increased the drive in women or if that had been some bit of junior high school lore that had remained uncorrected throughout his life causing him to imagine that her frustration seemed more overt than usual. Craig then remembered that he had made the decision. He had resolved the issue, finally, the night before, and celebrated his future celibacy by drowning his fears in the remaining bottles of homemade thimbleberry wine and homemade rum. His throbbing head was a testament as to how hard the decision had been and how hard it would be to stay true to that decision. He needed to stay strong, and backing himself slightly away from her under the sheets in order to cool down just a bit was one of the hardest things he had done in recent memory, but it was important. She would not understand, but he had decided for her too, and was glad that he had not gone through with his plan to show her some of the x-rated movies his brother had given him for her edification. The human race was to die with him, and now with her. He was not going to let a new wave of destruction, hate, and war arise from his genetic line. The Earth needed to heal and make way for the next race of animals to mature and perhaps steward the planet better. He would not have children. And the young naked woman, who could not even express her needs that consumed her in fits in his bed, didn't need the burden of caring for kids, when she could barely survive the Alaskan winters herself. Funny, he thought, how he always imagined such problems would disappear with his age nearing seventy. He certainly could not picture his grandparents having to worry about doing anything in bed.

Suddenly all his thoughts stopped. Time had passed, she had turned entirely around in bed, Craig's sheets were damp, and the sun and light in the room had moved positions. But he had not slept, nor dreamed. It was as if he just blinked, and a part of the day had disappeared. He tried to sit up, but he was too weak, and sore. He felt as if he had just run a long distance, and had fallen off of a cliff, beating up his muscles on rocks on the way down. What had happened?

"I think I had a seizure or something," Craig said out loud to her as panic gripped him. She looked at him intensely, staring, as if wanting to communicate that something had happened. Quickly quitting the attempt, she grabbed him and held him close, kissing his neck, and moving the cold sheets. She stroked his hair and cooed lightly. He did feel slightly better that she was with him, even if she knew nothing about medicine, or emergencies, or even human anatomy. Just knowing that she had been there with him lessened his anxiousness as he struggled to figure out what had happened and what he needed to do. He had seen hundreds of seizures as a nurse, especially when he worked in group home settings. They were common for people with epilepsy, but he did not have the condition. Maybe he was sick, or maybe something had been wrong with the homemade booze he had consumed all night. It was hard for him to diagnose himself without any tools, and with so much pain in his head.

She began again to pulsate her body against him and on top of him, forcefully. Craig held her close to stop her movements. He needed her. It was tangible, her being with him. He realized that this caring companionship was an important thing he had been missing all those years when he lived alone in silence. Was that love? Knowing that someone would be with you? He wasn't sure, but it did not seem to be enough to stir people to poetry and marriage. But this was a bad episode, and he needed her. He felt that he needed her more than anyone or any other thing at this moment. He was suddenly weak. His head throbbed with each heartbeat. Craig's fear of the headache made him shake, and he did not want to remember. Now, he had no choice. This was bad.

The first time he heard about the Disease, it was that glorious time Craig looked forward to after the long, busy, Alaskan winters. He had learned to make a living putting his degrees to use working as a medical consultant, and traveling as needed throughout the State. It was the perfect job for him with the built-in excuse of travel keeping him from ever getting close to people, most of which he disliked simply for being human. He always reserved the summer months for himself, to relax and live without deadlines in the woods near the Haines Highway. The year before the summer of the Disease had been particularly busy and he had decided not to talk or see anyone during his summer vacation time. Over the winter he had stocked up on all the food and beer he would need for the summer. Once he made it to his cabin, he diverted his mail, directed his telephone to a voicemail system, and discontinued his Internet service. He wanted the time to be his own, making no contact with anyone, with the options of sleeping late, not bathing, drinking too much, and hiking the wilderness open to his whims at all times.

Within the first few weeks of the "Summer of Craig," a mantra he stole from an episode of Seinfeld, news of the Disease started to eat its way into the 24-hour news cycle Craig kept on in his cabin, brought to the wilderness through the magic of the little gray curved dish screwed to a pine tree and the fact that Newton had been correct predicting that the satellite that reflected the television signal back to his cabin would never fall from orbit. At first, stories of hospital services being overwhelmed by a new condition sweeping the country tended to be reported upon about once an hour, with the conspiracy pundits suddenly finding themselves in great demand. No one was sure what was happening. People were dropping dead quickly, at work, at home, and in their cars. One story was repeated non-stop about the couple that went to the movies only to end up dead in their seats before the credits rolled. It appeared that some agent had been poisoning people, and that the poison somehow quickly disrupted brain chemistry, making it impossible for the brain to send the signals that regulate muscles such as the heart or diaphragm that moves the lungs. It did not take long for panic to ensue. Craig watched the drama unfold in real time from his lens on the world in his cabin, as if it were some distant science fiction B-movie, too bizarre to be true.

At first, governments issued health warnings. People were told not to eat certain fish, then meats, especially the brains or nerves bundles of the animals. The unofficial list of possible causes of the Disease was extensive: vaccines, insecticides, preservatives, radio wave experiments, Mad Cow Disease, artificial sweeteners, fluoride in the water, global warming, aliens, and so on. After meats, the governments advised that milks and cheeses were to be avoided. One national pizza chain CEO refused to close his stores and could be seen on every network newscast offering free pizzas delivered to anyone if they only agreed verbally to buy one pizza at their regular price after the health scare was resolved. Before the pizza plan could get off the ground, the truth leaked out and a series of national curfews and quarantines were put in place.

By the time scientists pinned down the problem, it was virtually all that was on television, twenty-four hours a day. A never-before identified type of virus was found in all dead victims' brain tissue, and then in all live human brain tissue they tested, in samples that went back for years or perhaps a decade. Apparently extremely contagious, the virus quietly created massive copies of itself in the brains of humans and then became dormant as crystals in the head. For some reason, never really explained, a second, also extremely contagious virus triggered the revival and release of the first virus when it made it into the body. The second virus took months to reach a tipping point in the body, whereby the host wandered around his or her daily routine without feeling ill, spreading the disease to everyone they met within speaking distance. The second virus also had the uncanny ability to stay alive and active for weeks, if not months, on items such as doorknobs, ATM machines, mail, food containers, and gasoline pump handles. Death occurred when the second virus triggered the release of the first, and what was called a "Bloom" occurred in the head that attacked a extremely specific set of neuroreceptors creating a chemical imbalance that the body could not regulate quickly enough. The first symptom people ever noticed was an unstopping headache, sometimes followed by seizures or paralysis, sometimes followed by bizarre zombie-like walking around activity, but always followed by death. Quickly. Usually within a day.

Craig remembered how quickly society unraveled once the truth of the Disease was reported. Officially, most leaders of the world imposed quarantines on everyone. But there was no control. Armies dissolved as they too were quarantined from themselves. Travel stopped, banks closed, and stores were looted and cleaned out instantly until the little gasoline left on tap in cities was used up. Absolutely everyone that was tested was found to have already acquired both viruses. Both viruses were unstoppable by antiviral medications, and the work on vaccines and viral suppressants required more time than the time it would take for the inevitable to occur to the people doing the work. Everyone in the world realized that they were going to die or went crazy in denial as people dropped *en masse* everywhere a news camera was pointed.

Craig watched the destruction of society feeling an odd mix of terror and joy. It had been his fantasy hope that all people would just die and go away. But he never wanted to die along with them. Seeing events unfold, logically, he was forced to prepare for his own demise. He realized that he would never leave his home. With the Haines Highway being the only road from his little town, one direction led to the Canadian border 12 miles away, a border that was closed and would result in a bullet in his body if he tried to reopen it himself. The other direction led to Haines, 27 miles away, and stopped at the ocean. With the Alaskan Marine Highway ferry system suspended and the little airport shut down, there would be no escape that direction either, unless he stole a boat from someone and learned to sail it without gasoline in his last dying hours. But there was no point in going anywhere anyway. Everyone was dying, everywhere. He was sure that he had also picked up the viruses along with everyone else. He consoled himself that at least he did not feel bad, and that he had a good supply of food and beer to use up before the end came.

Craig could not stop watching as society and civilization ended on his television screen. People took to shooting and raping each other as the population dwindled and corpses lined the city streets. The non-stop newscasts became a series of grainy webphone footage documenting some building burning, some army aircraft crashing, some vigilante group murdering people, or some new official claiming control of the country and issuing curfew orders. He remembered that he would turn off the television and just watch the woods out of his windows. The sun still shone, the wind still blew, and the birds still sang. At his cabin, everything was fine. No one ever came calling, or even drove down the road near his cabin. All was fine and as it should have been, until he looked at the television programs.

After weeks of drinking binges and watching the satellite channels dwindle down to a few working stations, Craig felt that he had reminisced enough about his life and decided that it was a good thing that he and the rest of the population were on the way out. He was satisfied that he was lucky to witness the end, and if there were some afterlife, he would be special somehow having witnessed it. It felt like justice somehow, that the humans who had destroyed and killed so much as a species were being made to pay for their sins and would exist no more.

The last television station to stay on the air degraded programming to one camera continuously focused on a desk area in a newsroom somewhere in Atlanta. People would wander in and out, reporting some bit of news heard on a short-wave radio or by a friend of a friend with some access to some working communication device. Reporting usually started with some comment about almost everyone being dead and some personal revelation about the reporter-by-default's impending death. Craig learned that while the United States had fallen into leaderless anarchy, leaders of other countries took it upon themselves to use up their weapons and start the wars they had always desired to fight. Countries unleashed missiles and jet attacks on their own and adjacent peoples. Some nuclear weapons were reportedly exploded near China. Armies were mobilized. But in the end, everyone fell dead all around the world from the Disease just the same.

By the time the satellite television went off air for good, Craig was already rationing his generator usage. He wanted his supply of gasoline to last until his time came, which he estimated to be by the end of the summer at the latest. He found his old short-wave radio and listened daily for any new information. In the end, he cursed himself for using up all of his last remaining batteries to listen to static, never interrupted by voice or music. Craig watched the days and weeks go by, often in a semi-drunken state, waiting for the headaches and death to come. Each day, the sky grew more and more hazy, due to the dust in the atmosphere from the atomic explosions, Craig figured. As time passed, he imagined that the radioactive fallout was killing him just as surly as the viruses were. But by the time the first snows of September appeared, Craig realized that he had survived both killers, and was probably the last human on the planet.

Although the Disease had not killed Craig, Mother Nature almost did the job as swiftly. Having frittered away his summer, begging death to come in a beer-induced haze, when the chill of the Alaskan winter came, Craig found himself without the supply of firewood he would need. He had been forced to spend the winter cutting down frozen trees in ten-foot snow depths with a handsaw in the two or three hours of full light each day, and eating small snacks of beans or rice at night just to make it through. It was a much different life than the one that included travel, lectures, and restaurant meals he had planned for himself, but he was happy. How could he not be? He was alive. But he had doubted whether he could last, especially when summer never returned the next year.

Craig had heard about what was called nuclear winter, but knew very little about the theory. He did however acquire first-hand observations during the first year after the Disease. While the days grew longer to the point that his home and town were lit around the clock in June, the snow never fully melted. Even on clear days, the sky looked yellow, and the sun looked dark and angry. Salmon never came up the river and berries never formed. Soon after June, the snow started to fall again, and winter returned. Craig had collected the roots he could identify and the high bush cranberries left from the year before, and froze the trout and birds he was able to catch before the bitter cold returned. He praised himself for the foresight to store several 50-poind bags of rice from Costco in his cabinets. Each had only set him back about $20 in the time of money, but were literally worth the value of his life after the Disease had come. Day by day he survived. And in the end, the sky and the woods returned to normal. And everything was the same, except that he was the only human, and he was on his own. It turned out just as he had always hoped.

Now, the time had come to say goodbye to the life Craig had wanted. He could not deny it to himself. He must have somehow picked up the missing part of the Disease from her or her cabin, kept alive somehow after all those years. She was apparently immune, and he would have normally hated her for that fact, as he hated people in general. But he didn't. He had been prepared for death, had expected it, for nearly two decades straight. It was almost a relief that it had finally come. Was that love? Forgiveness and blamelessness? No. It seemed odd, with his head exploding, and death impending; all he wanted to know was if he could feel love.

Suddenly Craig was fully engaged with her. Through his intense pain, as if a fireplace poker had been pushed through his head, and in the dizziness, his confusion and dream-like memories were augmented by a warm, sexual pleasure that overtook him. She had straddled him and was thrusting on top of him, moaning loudly. He wondered briefly how she had known what to do and how he could have avoided it. The pleasure was powerful, overwhelming, and it forced out all other concerns. His body pulsated and he felt as if his limbs were filled with a flowing electric butter that bubbled with increased ecstasy with each thrust of her body towards his.

"No!" Craig shouted. "I decided. We can't. No! No!" He was weak. She was determined and in control.

"No…" she mimicked. "Noooo…"

Craig's bodily pleasure was building, and the joy had relieved his head pain enough to think. He resolved to stop this. He could not take the chance at starting up the human race again. It had to end with him.

"No…" she moaned in obvious enjoyment.

Then it happened. Craig realized that he loved her. Suddenly, what he wanted no longer mattered. She wanted him. And he only wanted whatever she wanted. He wanted to be with her forever. He wanted her to remember him forever. And suddenly, surprisingly, almost 70 years of cynicism melted. Quickly he calculated, as his memories and delusions burned out of control in his head. If there were even a chance that she could raise offspring as beautiful as she was, perhaps it was worth the chance of repopulating the world. A world of humans like her would be Eden. Craig felt feelings long lost: hope, trust, companionship, and physical pleasure, all rolled into one. He did love. Finally. He knew it. He loved her. He tried to keep that thought clearly present as he felt himself slipping away.

"Noooo…" she whispered loudly.

He held her close as she continued to thrust herself upon him and as the last of his genetic material was provided for her fertile womb. His consciousness slipped into confused and disjointed imagery, as his body melted into a warm, painless, afterglow bliss.

One last thought filled Craig's entire being, a thought that lasted forever. He felt love. Love of a human. Love of her. And that thought of love lasted timelessly for Craig, for all of eternity, as no other thought ever replaced it.

"No." she gasped, as her new life started without Craig, his face forever remembered in the profile of her firstborn son.

HIGHWAY TO HAINES

O ut of the soft warmth it came. Increasing loudness. An eternal shrillness. It commanded attention and ended the relaxedness of the dream reality.

"It must be morning," David's thoughts focused as he pondered the sound of the alarm clock. Something was wrong. The sound was off somehow.

"Aaauugh!" his voice reflected back in all directions adding to the deafening sound, now identified as a car horn. He had attempted to roll over to shut off the imagined morning alarm only to be racked throughout his body with a pain of incredible sharpness and intensity that almost forced him to loose consciousness again. What was happening?

Catching his breath and letting the sound of his continuously sounding Jeep horn wash over him, David was careful not to move the lower part of his body again. His body was pressed between the car seat and what was left of the steering wheel and dashboard. He was held tightly with cold metal pressing all areas, the sharp edges piercing his wet skin in too many places to count. The cold autumn air blew a light spray on his face from a small creek cutting along the snow-covered ditch through a gap in the metal that once housed a windshield. He suddenly remembered what had happened, shaking in terror as he fully realized his situation.

He had been driving home from the elementary school where he worked to complete practicum hours for his college classes. The drive back and forth to the school in Haines from his home in Mosquito Lake, 30 miles away, had always been a daily inconvenience. But now, in the icy Alaskan November cold snap, that inconvenience had become an hour-long test of nerves, edging his rusty Jeep around winding corners on sheets of frozen run-off and packed snow. This day, running late due to the slowness of the school buses, the fear of hearing his professor over the audio conference speaker phone make a snide comment about his not being responsible enough to join the class at the afternoon start time drove him to push the limits of the grip created by the somewhat worn metal studs on his old snow tires.

"I'm really late now," his cracking voice barely audible over the single metallic tone of the continuous honk. A slight smile appeared on his face as he realized that he might have to drop his class now and take it over at another time. What joy it would be if he were suddenly released from the impending doom of the upcoming class assignments that had little possibility of being accomplished by the end of the semester. The joy fleeted with sight of his leg, as David began to take stock of his situation.

Having spent the last sixteen years as a nurse, David had developed a good sense of body functions and limitations. He had already resigned himself to the fact that both of his legs and at least his right hip were fractured. He had felt that feeling before, the indescribable sense of wrongness and pain experienced when a bone was not hinged in the socket it had been born with. But it was the porcelain-white foot, bent to an impossible angle relative to his own, pinned torso, which triggered a professional panic and ignited a wave of adrenalin-induced call for quick action. More than the foot, which was arguably of no more use to him than a reminder of the life now gone forever, was the small river of bright red liquid flowing off of the end of the cold heel. The flow was unending, unslowing, and constant, creating an explosion of fear and panic that made thoughts spin and flee. The sight closed the entire world down to an emergency episode like one of the hundreds that he had experienced before. Emergency episodes were short, and did not always end well for the patient. He understood that all too well.

David moved his body probably no more than a quarter of an inch within the huge metal clamp that was his crushed half-ton vehicle before the pain forced his head back screaming. It was a physical impossibility to reach any part of his body near the severed artery because of the welded frame that was now twisted over his lower abdomen and legs. He needed a tourniquet. But even if he had one, where would he tie it? Around his chest? That wouldn't work. He couldn't even move his leg against anything to slow the flow of precious blood. This was bad, he thought, really bad. Taking a deep breath, he told himself not to panic. Think.

The loudness of the horn cleared his head and reestablished hope. "Okay," David said aloud, "I'm at about mile fourteen. That stupid curve, I always hated that one, I almost made it…" Suddenly, he felt himself somewhat sleepy, and closed his eyes. He imagined that the cold chill of his head and shoulders were becoming warmed by a soft blanket that awaited him at home.

"No!" he screamed, shaking his head awake. "Don't do this, don't do it! Help! HELP!!!" He could barely hear his own voice above the horn. The horn, that's right. Someone must be annoyed by now. Anyone that heard this endless blaring noise would want to investigate what was going on. He continued with his calculations. I'm at mile fourteen. That's probably too far for the guy who lives at the bend of the river at ten-mile to hear the horn. Klukwan village is at twenty-mile. But there are a few people that live just before the Bald Eagle Preserve, that's just a couple miles away! Surely they would be hearing the horn and coming to investigate.

Looking out of the metal jungle gym, David watched a Stellar Jay pick at the fallen leaves peeking out between snow sheets. No, he was kidding himself. Even if someone were on their way, and found him soon, there would be no way to get an ambulance here from Haines in time to replace the fluid draining down his lifeless foot. He knew how this emergency situation would end. He could hear the ambulance crew now, trying to make themselves feel better, saying, "He never had a chance…. He shouldn't have been driving so fast…. What was so important?" The fact that the accident was caused by a need to listen to a professor in

Anchorage talk about teaching five-year-olds how to spell the word "cat" correctly made the scene in his head all the more pathetic, and caused a tear to swell up in his eye, blurring the vision of the bright blue bird.

He was going to die. This was it. He had to do something! But what? There was nothing to do. Damn it, this was not fair! Dropping into his nursing habits, David looked at his skin, calculated his pulse and respiration rate. He judged the terrifying amount of blood that was dripping away into the dark underbelly of the crushed vehicle and estimated how much more could be spared. His pulse was high and his skin was getting pale. "I'd give myself about five or six minutes at this rate," he thought. "What do I do?"

Every thought was now precious. "These are the last things I get to think about, I can't waste them," David implored to himself. He had seen death so many times, probably hundreds of times. There was nothing impressive about it. One minute a patient was breathing, maybe even talking to you, the next, they were a piece of hard, cold ham, to be put in a big vinyl bag and sent away to a mortuary somewhere. There was no fanfare, no great light with angel music, nothing mystical about it. Just quiet, and cold, leaving a big, useless ham, just lying there. But now it was his turn and he needed it not to be the end of everything. Time was wasting, and he was wasting his last thoughts.

David was never one to really believe in any of the afterlife stuff that those crazy people tried to sell door to door in their white shirts and black pants. They always held pamphlets with pictures of white people with blond hair and blue eyes in puffy clouds, with a bearded old white guy stating that he made men out of dirt and women out of ribs. All those bible stories, turning people into salt, and making boats that held all the millions of life forms of the world, were obviously fiction. Besides, his first wife, who held a theology degree and read the bible in the original language, showed him how poorly translated The Book was anyway, and ruined for him ever being able to believe in any of it. But he needed a God now; maybe he should confess his sins or something. His thoughts began to slow as he closed his eyes again. Thinking of his bed at home again, again he felt the warmth of his blankets, pulled over his shoulders. He could almost smell his sheets as he thought, "Wouldn't it be great if there was a God?"

With a jerk, he opened his eyes. Something had changed. He cursed at himself, realizing how slow his brain was becoming as it took him a full ten seconds to realize that the endless death scream of his prized rusty Jeep had finally ceased. He could hear the running water of a nearby creek, and a soft bird squeal somewhere high. Maybe it was a sign from God. Now he was reaching. He had only a few moments, and he was wasting them. He needed to think of something. This was it, all the life he was ever going to get. "Look. Do something. Think!" he commanded himself. But he didn't know what to do. Again he thought of God. Remembering the movie *Gandhi*, David thought about the Hindu religion. He had read that by saying the name of God with your last breath, it ensures that you go to heaven. That made as much sense as any other religion's way to paradise, besides, there were more Hindu people in the world than any other group, so they must be right.

"Help!" he suddenly didn't want to be alone. It didn't make sense. He was feeling so tired. He just wanted someone to tell him…something. He couldn't think. He was never going to graduate now. He would never be a teacher, work for twenty years, and retire and be happy. It wasn't fair. He should have tried to be happy more often with the life he had. He needed more time, more life, and another chance. But he was so tired.

Panic gripped him. "This is it. This is my last thought! Oh, I love life, I love living. Don't make me stop." He forced himself to look. He looked at the sky, looked at his solid white limbs. Somehow, by being a witness, by seeing that the world does exist, it made his being there somehow important. But what was the point? He was about to die. Everything he had done, everything that had happened, was about to end. He was about to be a cold ham, ready for the big bag. Then, one day, the expanding and exploding sun would swallow up the world, and it will be as if none of it had ever happened. He needed to sleep. And it was so cold. And there was just no point for his ever having lived.

David closed his eyes…

Then things felt better. It was all fuzzy somehow, and there was a slight ringing in his ears, but it was okay. David could feel his blankets on his shoulders. It felt so good to be in his bed, at home, all safe and warm. The smell of his sheets filled his nose, and he could see the firelight through the door of the woodstove, telling him that he could sleep for a few hours before it would need another log. He was also in his Jeep somehow, the way it ended up, all twisted about. No, he could not move, but that was okay, he was warm and safe. The blood was just a trickle off the end of the cold frozen foot, still bent in a direction clearly not possible. He could not remember what it was that he was supposed to do, but it felt like it had been completed, whatever it was, and he felt better. It was as if he had finally completed a big paper for class, or as if he had just ended the last shift before a long awaited vacation. He was happy.

It was time to sleep. David tucked the sheet and blanket over nose and felt the warmth from the stove. He looked out through the two bent steel rods at the Stellar Jay, moving about, picking at the snow covered ground. It was the brightest, prettiest bird he had ever seen. The color was amazing, beautiful. The bird was the most incredible thing he had ever seen. He loved that animal, as he never loved anyone or anything in his life. "I'm going to sleep now, bird. You carry on now...I...I love you."

Tears rolled down his face, chilling the warmth from the stove. With sudden clarity, and with sudden awareness of his heavy, crushed body, pressed between metal, David could feel a tearing separation from alertness. The car was spinning. His vision narrowed to the center, as if all of the world were only a small television screen seen through a bright light tube. The warmth of his body changed to a liquid numbness, floating lightly on the waves of an endless warm sea. The racing, pounding beat in his chest that had been wildly attempting to maintain a flowing pressure of the oxygen-enriched lifeblood suddenly slowed to a rambling impromptu pattern. There was no return now. Even the command for filling the lungs had ceased from that old animal part of his brain, as the cells in his head fired in random sequence, illuminating memories long lost over the darkening tunnel vision before his eyes. His brain, his body, and all that was him-as-a-being called for sleep, and it would be the last thing the collection of cells known as "David" would ever do in unison. He called out; "It's your world now, bird. It's all yours...take care of it...for me...you are...God!"

All was quiet.

A small creek babbled while a bright blue bird moved about, pushing the snow with its beak. A light creak came from the mass of twisted metal, chrome, and broken glass, as the large piece of cold meat inside shifted, when the last bit blood drained away from it. Then, quiet, nothing but quiet.

IT HAPPENED ALONG THE HAINES

CARETAKER ON THE HAINES HIGHWAY

J erry was a little late getting to his office. Not that it would matter, and not that anyone but Mary would know. As the only State Trooper in the Alaskan borough the size of Delaware, there was little if any way for anyone to try and track his comings or goings, nor would there be any point. Essentially, he was at work 24 hours a day, and if anyone said anything, he could just mention the countless hours of uncompensated overtime that unions in other states he had worked in would have conducted strikes over. Still, Jerry liked to get to his office by 9 a.m., before the doors were opened by Mary for the rare DMV needs of the residents along the Haines Highway.

"Good morning, Mary," Jerry chimed brightly.

"Good morning, Officer Branson," came the monotone response. Jerry did not expect any more expression. It took months for him to become comfortable working around the Native Alaskan grandmother who rarely spoke and never mentioned any topic not related to official business. Jerry had heard from others how lively and fun Mary was during weekend activities, and wished he could see that side of her, just once, but finally decided not to hold it against her. Mary had one of the only State jobs in town other than the ferry dockworkers. Jerry learned to admire her constant single-mindedness in providing no reason that someone could to point to that could end up jeopardizing her future State retirement benefits that were promised during the oil-tax rich days after the pipeline had been built. One day, Mary would free from work and comfortably rich. Coming to Alaska later, Jerry's pathetic retirement plan was just one more reason not to get comfortable, and to keep his feelers out to other states before his income-earning years were over. If only he could really leave Alaska now, after coming so far.

Unlocking his small back room office and pausing in the creaky antique military-issue desk chair as the phone message alert light blinked at him slowly and insistently, Jerry reviewed in his mind, as he had done a thousand times before, the "vision" that had led him to this very job, in this very small town of Alaska. Maybe it was a dream, or maybe it was a hallucination. The memory of the vision was so embedded in his psyche that it was long past the point that he could remember it clearly or objectively. He had made the mistake of talking about it at one time, before the Academy, and had learned by scorn and ridicule that he could never speak of it again to anyone. It was his secret. The vision was a pact between God and him alone. Just thinking about it in those terms seemed silly, and made him smile. The whole reason for him being in Alaska was based on this idea that God was a separate being, and one that was capable of directing and changing his reality in a personal manner. Obviously, that was a crazy thought in this modern age. He was crazy. But he was a crazy man with a loaded gun at his side, and with a badge.

Jerry saw the vision in his head that was now a central tenant to his life. It was a flash, a voice, a set of directions, and a promise all at once. It had been in his head, but it was more. He still believed it; he *had* to believe in it. Jerry had been commanded to go to the Haines Highway in Alaska and become the "Caretaker." In reward, he would be given a home that he would own outright where he could live until he died. Opening his eyes, Jerry muttered, "Look at me now. Caretaker in Chief, of this mess…"

Jerry needed to get to work. He didn't really even want to work in law enforcement. Becoming a Trooper just fell into place while he was trying to figure out how to make a living and get relocated to the area. It was a long process, and he thought he would like it, but he felt like an imposter in the end. And he wasn't really sure if he could kill someone, even if was to save others. Fortunately he had yet to be tested in that area. Starting a new log and checklist for the day, Jerry mechanically moved through the required steps. He reviewed the unsolved items to watch for during the day. Not much had changed in the last few weeks. Most problems that presented themselves simply required Jerry to show up and act as a fair referee. Mostly, he had to be the parent that separated fighting family members or the doctor that told drivers to stop drinking and sleep it off somewhere. Jerry looked at himself in the cheap mirror under the American flag, and continued his daily checklist. Yes, his uniform was in order, and his gun was in working order. He had completed target practice only a few days earlier. Jerry mused at his reflection. He did look official and imposing, especially in the flat brimmed hat, dressed in the polyester dark colors, punctuated with gold insignia and black implements of every kind.

Jerry practiced his stoic stare and deep voice. "Please step out of the car. Exit the car now." He had learned how valuable it was to give short commands and never argue. When he arrived onto a problem, he was in charge. Then he sighed. How did it come to this? All he wanted was to have a home and relax. This job was far too serious for the long term, Jerry again realized.

Last item before heading out was to check the phone messages that he had successfully ignored until the last moment. The first two were the usual fare, and could have been easily imagined ahead of their playing. Some official worker in Juneau noted an incorrectly marked check box on a form and she needed Jerry to resubmit it. Headquarters called to inform Jerry that his vacation request would have to be changed again as there was a shortage of relief Troopers to cover his Borough in his absence. It was a good thing that Jerry had not made solid plans, he considered. Maybe he should wait until winter to try again? But the last message was something that would at least make the day different than most.

"Hi, uh, Jer. This is Raymond, Raymond Tyree, at the end of Mosquito Lake Road. You know, by the old

R.V. park. Anyway, hey, I found this briefcase, well, it is more of a suitcase, floating in Mosquito Lake. The thing is, it is made of some metal, like aluminum, and I think it is important. I'm here all day, and I'll be around all week. I think you should come pick it up and get it back to whoever lost it. Thanks."

Jerry had recognized Raymond's voice at the start. It was amazing how quickly he had learned so many of the names of the 2500 people that lived in his Borough. Raymond was a good man, and an "old timer" to the area. Jerry would at least enjoy chewing the fat with him, but he sighed again as he grabbed a blank copy of the "Found Item" report and turned out the lights to the office.

Jerry enjoyed the second half of each workday. It almost made it all worth it. Each day he was required to drive the Haines Highway from Haines to the Canadian border, to check for stranded drivers and to just make sure the State's presence was seen by the locals. The view along the drive was phenomenal, and he still appreciated the wild beauty of the Chilkat River bordered by the dramatic, sharp, snow-peaked mountains on both sides. Depending on his mood and the pending workload, Jerry would take the side roads from the highway into Klukwan to appear more approachable to the Tlingit Elders, over the bridge to Porcupine Creek to see if they were filming a "Gold Rush" episode, or down to the end of Mosquito Lake Road just to keep order. Mostly he liked to take the side roads to take in the local views. He also enjoyed checking in with the Border Patrol agents at the customs office. Even though those officers were

Federal law officials, it was fun to commiserate with fellow law enforcement minded people, far from big city concerns. The required drive could be done in as short as ninety minutes if needed, but Jerry enjoyed stretching the time to at least three hours, driving at 45 miles per hour to remind the other drivers who rarely dared to pass him in his large, officially decorated SUV, that it is safer to take the winding Haines Highway slowly, especially considering the blind corners and the number of bears and moose that also used the pavement to navigate the forest.

Jerry saved calling on Raymond for his return trip from the Canadian border, which marked the 40-mile limit of his charge from Haines. At mile 27, Mosquito Lake was considered an unincorporated town by the State, with about 300 people counted there during the 2010 census. In reality, the town was a three-mile road from the Haines Highway to the natural little lake, with homes tucked away in the woods along the stretch. There was a small school, a fire station, a wildlife zoo for tourists, and a one-room store along the road. The people that lived there had to be creative in making a living or had to travel to towns where jobs existed. Jerry marveled at the tall pines that lined the road and noted nothing unusual or changed in any way as he traveled the three miles to the end where Raymond enjoyed his retirement overlooking the small lake that currently supported two pairs of swans sharing the view.

Raymond was out of his house and walking to Jerry's SUV before he could turn the engine off. Such an approach would normally make Jerry nervous as a challenge to his control, but he knew Raymond and was glad he wouldn't have to spend time trying to track him down in the woods.

"I've got it right here. Look at it!" Raymond started, hefting the large aluminum case to the height of his head, blinding Jerry briefly as it reflected a large slosh of the midday sun in his eyes.

"That's some fish you caught there, Ray. Did the game warden have to check your license for a suitcase stamp when you hauled that out?" Jerry returned smiling, exiting his SUV as he placed his hat and checked his utility belt automatically.

"It's all locked up tight, and pretty heavy. But it floats. I can't tell how you open it. Look here. See this engraved part here at the bottom, next to the lever that releases something up front. I don't know what it is supposed to mean, but it sure looks like it's military to me." Raymond cradled the large case upside down with both arms while Jerry studied the engraved code numbers. The Trooper could see now why the man had been excited about his find. It was very unusual and expensively crafted. It certainly was not the daypack for sweaters and sandwiches that tourists carried as Jerry had imagined during his previous slow drive.

Jerry wrote down the details of the find as Raymond told the tale with large dramatic gestures, in the same manner Jerry had witnessed Raymond use to tell his story of a record halibut catch during his youth. The metal case was found at the headwater area of the lake, before the campground, where the little creek came down a steep canyon, and where no one lived. Raymond had already asked around, and checked the campground, but no one was camping there. No one he had talked to was missing such a case.

Jerry thanked Raymond, placing the suitcase in the passenger seat and latching the handle with the seatbelt. "You know Ray, I think that you have a right to whatever is in there if no one claims it in a few months."

"No way. That thing has got to be military. I don't want to get involved with anything that is going to mess up this little life I've got going here. But tell you what; if there's something valuable in there and no one wants it, we can split it. But don't put my name on it anywhere. In fact, why don't you take my name off that little report you wrote there. I want to be anonymous." Raymond suddenly looked serious as he pointed to the half-finished report Jerry had started.

Jerry thought about it for a second, and realized he was going to have to make a new report anyway, on the computer. Plus, he had taken the notes he needed on his pocket pad, without Raymond's name connected to the find. He handed the sheet to Raymond as he started backing away. "Here you go, Ray. Light your stove with that. You are now just an unnamed citizen doing your civic duty." Jerry nodded once, in his most official-looking manner as the smiling man waved his half-completed document, no doubt to be saved as physical proof of some future tall-tale to be constructed for the enjoyment of visiting grandchildren.

Jerry headed back to the highway, stopping at the campground to visualize where the metal monstrosity had been located. There were no campers, as there almost never were. Jerry had always surmised that the name "Mosquito" dissuaded all but the most brave from enjoying the clean little camp and dock, although the name was quite apt at times. Since the creek came rushing down the fairly steep canyon into the lake at this point, the flow of the water moved away from the camp area to the large part of the lake a half of a mile away. From where he stood, he could see the flow, almost as a river more than a lake at the small end. He could see leaves floating past him and Jerry considered that it didn't take Sherlock Holmes to realize that however the case ended in the water, it had happened at the upper end, because the case could not have floated upstream. Returning to his SUV, popping a couple ripe blueberries in his mouth from the bushes that lined the shore as he walked, Jerry produced a plat map of the area he had the borough office copy off for him. Jerry briefly considered that maybe he was right for this job after all, preparing ahead of time with maps was pretty smart, and he had to admit, little mysteries like this were fun to solve. It might even be important.

The map showed Jerry that there were few properties that were close to the top part of the lake. Most of the land was part of the campground or was State land that was the protected watershed of the lake. Above the start of the lake where the creek entered the canyon, there were two properties across the road. After that the school held the rest of the land until one passed over the next ridge. Across from the school was the short dirt road named Riverside that circled back to the lake where a couple properties bordered the lake near the upper part. In all, Jerry figured that four properties were close enough that the people living there might have seen something. He made a quick plan, and decided to stop by each, in order, from the campground, and only briefly, before heading back to Haines for the night.

Heading up the hill about a half of a mile, the first property to the right had a long dirt driveway, across from where the creek entered the canyon out of view from the road just to the left. Jerry entered slowly but revved his engine loudly so that the owners knew he was coming. He knew that the widow Elizabeth lived there, and that at every coincidental meeting with her, she informed Jerry that she had a standing policy to shoot all trespassers first before asking questions. He knew it was her way of posturing for anyone who was listening, as she lived alone, but he believed her enough that he wanted not to surprise her just to talk.

Before he could drive up to the log cabin, sure enough, Elizabeth was standing in the pathway, with shotgun close but leaning against a small four-wheeler. "Afternoon Liz. You're looking good," Jerry started from his opened window.

"What are you looking for, Officer?" Elizabeth returned.

Jerry decided to stay in the SUV, but he turned off the engine. "Wow, look at this place. You sure have added on lately. That garage looks great. And look at that deck."

"Thanks. *We've* been working hard, not that it's any business of yours. The assessor has already been around last year."

Jerry decided not to press who the "we" was, even though that was pretty big news in this little town. He could find out the whole scoop from the storeowner later. "I'm just out asking everyone if they've seen anything unusual lately and if they know anything about this big silver case that was found," Jerry continued in his friendliest tone, pointing to the case in the passenger seat.

"Nope, nothing going on around here," Elizabeth said, relaxing and shaking her head, lifting to her tippy-toes to see the case in the tall vehicle. "I've never seen that before. But you should talk to Ken down there," she continued, pointing downhill to the next property over.

"Why, what going on at Ken's?"

"Oh I don't know. I mean, I haven't seen anything, but he is weird. I don't think he has a job. But he's always got some scheme or another to try to make money. And sometimes, he just shows up at my door, trying to get me to sell something or another for him. One day, you'll get a call to come scrape his dead body off of my property. See those 'No Trespassing' signs? That means I am warning him, and I'll shoot him if I feel threatened..."

"Okay Liz, I get your meaning. I planned to talk to him next. Thanks for your time. I'll see you in town. Try to keep from shooting anyone for a while okay? The paperwork is a pain in the ass for shootings." Jerry smiled as he turned around. He wasn't sure if Elizabeth appreciated the joke or not, until she broke a slight smile that Jerry noted out of the side of his eye and confirmed it in the rearview mirror as he left.

Next stop was the property owned by Ken Thomas. His blue and brown house with the large Alaskan flag out front was near the road, and one of the few houses that could be seen on the way to the lake. Two cats scattered as Jerry got out of the driver's seat, jingling as he adjusted his belts. Ken's head popped up out of a garden of potato rows, hidden by high grass and highbrush cranberry plants. He slowly walked out and over to Jerry who stood fixed at the SUV. Ken was taller than Jerry, about six-four, but skinny as a pole. Jerry was reminded of Abraham Lincoln as Ken approached, the comparison completed by Ken's scraggly beard. Ken didn't say anything, which Jerry considered unusual, but he concluded that it might have something to do with the can of Olympia Beer in Ken's hand, and the stack of empties by the front steps.

"Am I being arrested?" Ken started as he unhurriedly moved to conversation distance with Jerry.

"Why, did you do something wrong?" Jerry paused, watching the thoughts being processed in Ken's head. "Just kidding Ken. Relax. I'm here just to ask a few questions. I need your help."

Ken was obviously relieved. He bounded over, smiling. Slurring his speech a little, he loudly started in, "Oh hey Jer, anything I can do to help, you know me. You had me goin' there for a second. I've done a lot of things in my day, you know. But I've been good, really. What do you need?"

"Have you seen anything unusual lately? Seen anything around here?"

"Well, let me see. Those Cooper kids sure do tear around on their four-wheelers. They go too fast down the road, gonna kill themselves one day. And they spend time hanging out at the school next door, especially at night. Oh and that woman up there is constantly building now that she's got a new man. It's all I hear, pound, pound, pound." Ken seemed to be enjoying himself, having someone to talk to and being taken seriously. Jerry knew that Ken was considered somewhat of a local character. Most people added that they could only stand to be around Ken for short periods of time when they spoke about him.

"That's all pretty interesting. Take a look at this. Do you know anything about this suitcase?" Jerry pointed to the bright silver canister in the front seat as he asked.

Ken visibly gulped. He instantly became pale as he stepped back slightly. Jerry was immediately taken that Ken did not try to get a better look to identify it. It appeared that he had seen it before and wanted to get away from it. Or was it the beer? Jerry did not want to prejudge Ken, the way others appeared to do.

Ken started, "No. No. I've never seen that. Why would you think I would know about that thing? Everyone always blames me for stuff." Ken stared at the case, transfixed, slightly swaying, with his skin color changing from pale to brightly flush. Jerry watched him for several moments as Ken stared in silence. It was very unusual, but it was so unusual he could not tell if the cause was guilt. He certainly indicated something, but maybe it was his reactions that made him seem unusual to others. Then, as if a switch had been thrown giving Ken electricity, he suddenly became animated and started talking rapidly, "People are always getting down on me because I got to make a living. I'm trying to stay here, you know. I got to keep making house payments but there's no work. But I don't let that get me down, I just keep goin'. I got lots of things goin' on. I sell stuff. I trade. There's the Internet stuff. And I work under the table sometimes. But I'm no thief. I don't steal."

Jerry slowed him down, "Whoa Ken. I'm not saying you're a thief or anything. I just have a mystery here and wondered if you could help me out."

"Right, yeah. No. I don't recognize that thing. I don't know anything. You know, if people got to know me, they would see that I'm trying to keep them happy. I'm trying to keep this town alive. In fact, if it weren't for me, the whole world would be in trouble. People owe me…" Ken continued talking until he rediscovered the opened beer in his hand.

"Well, I'm not really following you there, Ken. But are you okay? You know you can tell me anything." Jerry was half hoping that Ken did not have more to say.

"Sorry Jer. I didn't know you were coming or I wouldn't have started drinking. Oh hey, where are my manners? You want one. I've got a whole case coolin' in the creek over there. I won't tell anyone 'cause I know you're working." Ken had returned to his previous affect, smiling and animated.

"Thanks, no. But I'll take you up on that another day, okay? Are you sure that you don't know anything about this suitcase?" Jerry tried one last time. Ken denied any information. But Jerry noticed a pronounced frown on Ken's face as he drove away from the yard, scattering the cats again. The frown remained unbroken even when faced by Jerry's smile and wave as he left.

The Trooper pulled into the parking lot of the empty two-roomed school that was closed for the summer to refer to his map again. He looked at the plats on the off-chute dirt road named Riverside and realized that of the possible occupied lots that might have witnesses, only one property had a house that people lived in. He gathered his calm and drove to his next destination: The Coopers'. Pulling into the yard, Jerry mused that the family must be starting a four-wheeler ATV car lot. He counted five, and wondered how many more were in the barn with the backhoe parked in front. Jerry felt as if he were physically slapped, as a wave of diesel and gas fumes struck him while he proceeded to the door. He found a large doorbell button, which seemed out of place on the rough-honed cabin structure. But ringing the bell brought about the intended result of being surround by the residing couple in their forties, followed by several teenagers, all excited to hear what the important visitor wanted. After a round of "Yes sir" and "No sir" to opening questions, and repeated reassurances that the rambunctious young men were not in trouble, Jerry had the family (who obviously did not want him to enter) follow him to his vehicle to look at the silver case, not nearly as blinding to look at in the shade of the tall pines that surrounded the compound.

"Cool!"

"Is that silver or steel?"

"What's in there, a bomb?"

"That looks like the one in that movie, that had that laser gun in it."

Everyone in the family denied noticing anything out of place lately. Everyone denied knowing to whom the metal briefcase belonged. Jerry decided that the family members were all sincere, and only the oldest of the boys offered up no suggestions. He also did not state that he wished that he did have information that could help. Jerry was struck by the one question the eldest sibling did venture, wondering if there would be a reward if he knew anything that would help. Later, while Jerry drove slowly the 27 miles back to his office in Haines, he felt more convinced that there was something the oldest of the Cooper boys wanted to tell him, but couldn't, because he was in front of his family.

As soon as Jerry reached the point where clear radio contact was possible on the Haines Highway, he heard the call: "AK 045. AK 045." Well, that was the end to his hope to catch an early dinner and get in a couple hours of fishing before bed. If dispatch couldn't wait for him to return, there was a problem pending that could not be cleared quickly.

"AK 045. Over"

"AK 045, be advised, I've been asked to contact you as soon as possible to have you return a call to Juneau. Do you want me to patch you through now? Over."

"Thanks Dispatch. Message received. But I'm almost to town now. I'll call from base in a few minutes. Over."

"Ten-four."

Jerry surmised he was correct in his pending loss of free time by the ease at which he was able to talk to the Captain when he called without the usual round of phone-tag messages. "Jerry, I've been getting calls all day about a missing person, a Dr. Frank Kelly. Fifty-eight, gray hair, short cut, 5 foot 11 inches. He was on his way from down south to Anchorage, but decided to lay over in Juneau. From here he purchased a round trip ticket to Haines on a local carrier, uh, Tailwinds, and he flew in last Wednesday. But he didn't take the flight back. Apparently, he is an important scientist or something. I think he might be associated with the military, or some spy outfit or corporation. Whatever it is, I can't get a straight answer on anything about him. But we are supposed to keep it quiet and not list it as an official missing person at this point. I'm getting calls from everywhere. Even from both Senators' offices, so it is even a bipartisan concern to find this guy. I want you to see what you can dig up. See if he is still there, or maybe he just drove to Anchorage and got lost. I might have to send someone up, but see what you find out. Just keep it quiet."

Jerry didn't like the feel of it. He had received orders that were not orders, with possible military connections. It was the second time he had heard about possible military connections in one day, and he wondered if this Dr. Kelly was connected to the large metal case, as he pushed it in the closet and covered it with a blanket. He couldn't fit the thing in the safe, but he figured the case would be secure enough locked in his State office. He'd never lost anything from his office before. He would have to write up the Found Item report later.

Jerry started with the local Haines police department. He quickly learned that there had been no recent arrests, no missing people, and no medical emergency evacuations out of town. No reports on a Mr. Kelly, or a Frank, at all. Next, Jerry drove the three miles up the Haines Highway to the flat area by the Chilkat River that held the small plane runway. The short building at the end of the parking area with the large chipped paint cloud-shaped letters that spelled out "Tailwinds" contained 6 seats, a couple vending machines, and a counter area, all of which were covered with boxes of mail and packages of every sort.

"Sorry officer, the mail plane just got in. No passengers today, so we got our backload of junk mail. Can I help you?" The smiling blonde woman with an ID card in plastic clipped to her front top strap asked.

Jerry started in, asking about Wednesday, if she had been working, and if she remembered the gray-haired man, now needing to be found.

The woman was excited to be helpful. "I remember him. He was very odd. Not very nice either. He wanted to know why there weren't any taxis waiting at the airport so he could just hop right in. You know how tourists get. They don't realize how small the town is if they just fly in from somewhere. So I called him a taxi from Lady's Taxi, and even told him how lucky he was that she was in business and how we had no taxi service for about a year before she started up. But he wasn't very nice. All he did was sit and scribble on a big pad of paper. It was covered with little tiny notes and arrows, and numbers everywhere. He never thanked me or anything. So, you're the new officer I've heard so much about. Do you ever get any time off for fun?"

Jerry thanked the woman and had to explain that yes, he was single, and yes, he did get time off, but that it was hard to go to the bar and hang out on the weekend, being that he had had so many tense encounters with the people that tended to frequent the watering hole. He definitely was intrigued by the woman's offer to spend time with her at some point. He agreed to one day stop in again, a fair trade for the information. But for now, Jerry was actually enjoying his job. It was as if he were playing detective, but playing for real. He rarely embraced his occupation. How could he not think this was fun?

Jerry caught up with Hank, the taxi driver, at the ferry terminal, after calling the owner Lady at Lady's Taxi, which was her real name. Hank was working Wednesday, and would have been the only one to give Dr. Kelly a ride. While waiting for the Fairweather ferry to slowly edge to shore, Jerry sat in the passenger seat of the long white van in front of the terminal and listened to Hank recount the fare. "I like to meet the ferries when they come in. It costs a little gas to drive out here from town, but it is usually worth it. Seems like there are always a couple tourists who walk-on and don't realize that the ferry doesn't actually dock in town. If I'm not here, they catch a ride in with locals who are willing to help. It is kind of like fishing..." After some prompting from Jerry, he continued. "Yeah, I gave that guy a ride.

Quiet guy, didn't talk much. He kept writing down notes, like he was trying to finish a crossword puzzle or do his math homework or something. Is he okay?"

"What makes you ask that?" Jerry said remembering that he was to keep the concern about Dr. Kelly's quiet.

"Well, he didn't want to go to town, like most people would, to get a motel room or something. He wanted to go directly to the little Mosquito Lake School. He didn't look like an outdoorsman, and he didn't have a coat or any gear or anything. All he had were his notes and a big metal briefcase."

Jerry inhaled his saliva and coughed, he was so excited. "Was the briefcase about so big, and silver, with a rounded, long, black metal handle?" Jerry begged gesturing the size.

"That's the one. He said that he was meeting someone who ran a therapy retreat. Something to do with increasing brainpower. I'd never heard of any retreat up there, and I usually know what's going on, driving taxi. But he seemed pretty sure of himself. And kinda rude about it. I felt bad, just leaving him there in the parking lot 'cause the school is closed for summer. He'd have to walk two miles back to the highway where the store was if he didn't meet his contact. I know there are bears up there too. He said he'd be fine and gave me a twenty-dollar tip. I felt bad, like I said, but it was cruise ship day, and I had to get back to town to shuttle the tourists around. If I didn't get the tourist fares, my week would have been shot, and Lady would have been mad. Is he okay?"

Jerry didn't want to lie, but he didn't want Hank to feel bad, or start spreading rumors, which seemed like something that would be impossible to stop at this point. "Hank, I think he's fine. I've just got business with him, if you know what I mean. Could you do me a favor and keep it between us that I was asking about him? I don't want it to get out."

"Sure thing. You just keep driving the highway the way you do. I always feel better knowing that you go out the road at least once a day, in case I need help. And half of my business in the winter comes from you guys telling people they need to call a cab or go to jail for a DUI. So I won't say a word."

Jerry was almost shaky with excitement. The day had gone from the usual boring start that begged for his resignation to his investigating his first possible homicide. He decided that he had to know what was in the metal briefcase. He would claim later that he was looking for clues if questioned. He just needed to make sure he didn't disturb any fingerprints that might be on the inside. With crowbar and hammer in hand, Jerry unlocked his office, feeling grateful that it was after hours and that he would be alone in the building. As he suspected, it took many minutes of loud pounding to finally pry open the lid. Then, using his full weight on the crowbar to act as a lever, he popped the hinging apart, opening the briefcase fully open flat.

The case was empty. Jerry's heart sank. The interior was covered with a thick velvet-like material, which acted like very thick, stiff padding. There would be no fingerprints on the material, but he figured that he should close it anyway just in case. He wrapped the case back up in the blanket and hid it again in the back of the closet. It didn't matter. He had his witness that placed Dr. Kelly by the creek at the top of Mosquito Lake with the case. The case ended up at the start of the lake. So, something happened to Dr. Kelly between the school and the creek. Suddenly, Ken's earlier reaction to the case seemed too suspicious. Jerry wondered if Ken would still be awake, considering how many beers he had started on when Jerry had questioned him. He would have to head back to Mosquito Lake. In the summer, it stayed light until midnight, so there was no problem getting there. It just couldn't wait.

Before he headed out, Jerry opened the Internet browser on the fast new computer with State identification tags cemented to each side that had recently arrived unexpectedly after the budget was approved. Jerry tried several Google searches: Mosquito Lake resort, Mosquito Lake treatment, etc. It was not until he added the word "intelligence" that the site he was seeking jumped to the top of the list. It was a basic, pre-made business website, but it put all of the pieces together. The site claimed that a "special geological construct" located at Mosquito Lake provided a natural method for inducing a dreamlike state allowing for "conscious lucid dreaming" that "unlocked superhuman thinking abilities." The site was light on details but provided pages of testimonials from customers who had solved all of their life problems in just one session. Without any proprietor names, Jerry compared the telephone number listed to a reverse lookup page in the thin local phonebook to find the author: Ken Thomas, Mosquito Lake Road.

Jerry informed dispatch where he was going, in case something went wrong. He had no proof Dr. Kelly made it to Ken's house, or that they met, so Jerry needed to be smart. Maybe he could get Ken to confess. As Jerry drove the 27 miles of the Haines Highway back to Mosquito Lake, full speed this time, he tested and retested his pocket voice recorder to determine the best place to keep it on his body as he questioned Ken. Jerry slowed as he approached the Mosquito Lake School, with the next property on the road being Ken's. He noticed two of the Cooper boys with their four-wheelers next to the school and decided to stop and play a hunch first, since Ken could not see the SUV from his house.

"We weren't doing anything," the younger brother blurted. Both boys had jumped on their ATVs when Jerry stopped and walked over. "We were just playing."

"That's good, uh, Tom, right? Look Tom, I need to talk to your brother here. I need you to drive home. Your brother will be there soon, if he helps me," Jerry ended sternly, looking directly at the older young man. Tom didn't talk any more, and looked over his shoulder twice as he headed down the dirt road, not quite making it all the way to his house from the sound of the motor. Turning to the older brother, Jerry used his practiced grim expression, deep voice, and menacing stance. "Richard is your name, I'm told." Jerry waited for a little nod. "I know you know something about that metal briefcase I showed you. Now I need to know the truth. It is illegal to lie to me. I don't want you be in trouble.

There is no reward, but if you cooperate, you will have my appreciation, and I will owe you a favor. Okay? Talk!"

With the last command, the young man teared up and words rushed forward, with gasps for breaths in between. "I didn't want to tell you 'cause I don't want to go to jail. But if I don't do it, it gets so cold. An we don't have any money..."

"Slow down. What were you doing?" Jerry prodded, less intimidatingly.

"Over there. I was siphoning off some of the heating oil out of the school garage tank. Just one gallon or so. I was behind the fireweed, so no one could see me. That's when I saw that suitcase. There was an old guy sitting on the step who had it. He was waiting until Mr. Thomas came over and walked with him to his house over there."

"So you saw a man with the metal case go with Ken to his house?"

"That's all I saw. I don't want to get in trouble. I won't take any more oil, I promise. Don't tell my parents I told you. Please."

"Okay. Thank you for telling me Richard. I want you to go home now. If you don't take anymore oil from the school, I'll let it go. That's the favor I told you I would give you as a reward. There may be a time when I need you to tell that story to someone else, but you won't get in trouble, okay? Alright, thanks. Now get going."

Jerry sat in his SUV to think. Ken was now placed with Dr. Kelly and Dr. Kelly was missing, with his possessions scattered. He had every right to pull Ken in to question him, and he would. But first, he had to try something. Maybe Ken would slip and give himself up. He certainly wasn't very skilled at hiding his emotions, as when he saw the briefcase. It shouldn't be hard. But it could end badly, Jerry considered, making sure he had both his mace and handcuffs secured and ready for use. Suddenly, the old pang hit him. Was this really who he wanted to be? He really only wanted the promised home that he could just live in, without worries. He didn't want to be the macho cop, hauling in murderers, kicking and screaming. But it was too late. He was in it deep. "Here we go," Jerry told himself.

Jerry waved, rolling straight up the drive to the front porch where Ken was sitting, his long, pencil-thin legs brightly untanned and dangling over the side. There was a larger pile of empty beer cans than before, but Ken appeared fully awake and functioning. Jerry exited the SUV lazily and started, "Hey Ken. How's it going. That offer still good for a cold one?"

Ken stared, as in disbelief for a moment, then jumped to his feet and proclaimed, "Hell yeah! I've got plenty. I've even got more upstairs, but it'll take a while to cool off. I could throw them in the creek too if you want."

"Well, that's okay, I think. Let's see how the first one... or two go down," Jerry said, adding a smile that seemed to please Ken even more.

"Hey, did you ever find a home for that metal thing you were lugging around?"

"Nah. I just threw it in the lost and found. Maybe someone will claim it someday. Not my problem. But that's kind of why I came over. While I was asking around, someone told me about this thing you do that helps people think out problems. That sounds really interesting and I could use it."

Ken handed Jerry an ice-cold can, not smiling anymore. He shook his head and claimed, "I don't do that anymore. Gave that up a while ago. It was an Internet thing, and it made some money. But no more."

Jerry continued, "Aw, I heard it was a real thing. It helped a lot of people I heard. At least tell me about it. Come on." Jerry smiled again, and took a long pull off of the freshly opened beer. "I'd love to hear about it. I've got no where to go."

It was all that Ken needed to hear. He couldn't help himself. Someone was at his house, someone important, and he wanted to hear Ken talk. "Okay, I'll tell you. It is the coolest thing. Do you know anything about alpha waves? No? Well, your brain has these waves that happen when you think. There are different waves when you sleep and other ones when you dream. I read all about them after I found it. Anyway, you can sync up sounds that make the waves happen or change the waves. They do it in experiments, they make a certain wave in one ear and another in the other ear, and the waves combine to make long cycling wave that make you dream or sleep or whatever. It makes sense, I'm not explaining right, but it is real."

"Man, Ken, how many beers have you had? That sounds pretty far out there. I was hoping to get some help with my problems," Jerry said, thinking that he could keep him talking by challenging him.

"No, it's true! I would have never believed it until it happened to me. The first time, I sat down and stayed there for almost two days straight. It was great! You fall into a trance, kind of. But it is better. It's like you are dreaming but you are awake. You can do anything. So after I found it, I thought, well, I could have people pay me so that they could solve their problems, and then I could afford to live here."

"You have got to let me do that. It sounds crazy but great. What do you do? Take drugs or something?"

Ken stopped. Jerry could see that he was trying censor himself. Jerry held his breath and tried to look like he was hanging on every word. Ken started again slowly, "Is that really why you are here? I mean you are a cop right? Are you trying to entrap me into something?"

Jerry replied quickly, trying to get Ken rambling again, "No, I'm not on the clock. Can't be, I'm drinking. Tell me what this magic thing is. I'm really interested. Really. It must be something pretty big."

Ken grinned and said, "It is really cool. It's right over there across the road, in that canyon above the lake. There's something magic about how the water roars against the slate cliffs on both sides. It knocks you right into a dream. Especially if you have had a drink or two, or drink some valerian tea."

"How did you make money with that?" Jerry asked.

"People would pay me and I would take them over and make sure they were safe and had things they needed. Sometimes I had to shoo off bears. It worked better if they had paper and pencils, or something to record with. Sometimes they would talk and talk, working on stuff in their minds. Afterwards they remember what they saw, but they didn't remember me, or that they were talking. You want to go see it?" Ken asked.

"Would I? Let's go!" Jerry said, jumping to his feet. Ken talking about providing recording devices reminded Jerry to turn on his recorder, mentally yelling at himself for forgetting because he had stopped to talk to Richard at the school.

Ken led Jerry down to the road and down a steep slope to a fairly swift two-foot deep creek. Unlike Ken, in a tee shirt, shorts, and tennis shoes, Jerry, in his full uniform, slippery dress shoes, and implements all around snagging on shrubs and weeds, fell several times. Jerry realized he would have difficulty catching Ken if Ken made a break for it. He felt like he needed to wrap up this attempt for confession soon and get Ken in to a controlled environment where he could be questioned correctly. But that would bring the investigation to a fully official level, the way it really should be despite his orders from Juneau.

The closer they got to the top of the canyon down to the lake, the more Jerry noticed a loud pulsating sound. It was more than sound, it was a feeling too. It felt as if all of his muscles, his whole body, were being rolled in a rhythmic machine. It was soothing, and hypnotizing. By the time they had reached the point at which the water rushed over an edge to the lake below and started rapid slapping waves against the sheer solid rock walls rising high on both sides, the air was engulfed in a roaring wave of sound rushing from the right side to the left, followed by another wave, over and over, endlessly. Jerry felt too weak to stand suddenly, yet he was also overwhelmed with physical pleasure. It felt as if many people were giving Jerry a full massage over his entire body. There were two lounge chairs appropriately place, and Jerry quickly found one.

"Quite the experience, huh?" Ken said loudly to be heard over the rushing water. "It is hard to fight if you are not used to it. You just stay there until you are used to it."

Jerry agreed. He should stay there. He had to admit, there was something going on. He was physically impacted somehow. Jerry looked at Ken who was walking rapidly back and forth on a plank of wood that crossed the creek at the edge, singing to himself, with wide gestures. It had not occurred to Jerry until that moment that maybe Ken was actually crazy. Panic ensued briefly, but then he felt soothed again, reflexively from the sound. Was it really this creek thing or was he the one going crazy? Jerry then noticed that Ken was wearing bright orange earplugs. Maybe that would help. While Ken wasn't looking, Jerry produced his own earplugs still in his pocket from target practice the week earlier, and pushed them deep in each ear.

Ken spun around quickly. "I know why you are here, you know. You weren't fooling me. But now that you are here, I can tell you what happened. That scientist guy, Dr. Kelly, with that big metal case, he was here. And you figured it out somehow. I should have known that damn suitcase would float. I'm an idiot!"

Ken was pacing back and forth on the eight-inch plank waving his arms as he confessed.

"It's okay Ken. I'm sure whatever happened, it wasn't your fault," Jerry shouted, not sure how loud he was talking with the earplugs placed.

Ken yelled back, "It was. I did it. But you don't understand why. I had to. I had no choice. That guy was crazy. Remember when I told you that people who come here and slip into lucid dreaming to work out their problems, that they talk out loud? They write things down too. That doctor guy was crazy. You know what he was working on while he was here? He was inventing a disease that he was going to use to kill everyone. Only his problem was that he wanted to make it so that it only killed most of the people, and didn't hurt the ones he wanted to live. It was real. He really, really was doing it. And while he was here, he figured it out. The problem he had. He finished his disease, and was going to leave here and go out and kill us all. I'm serious."

Jerry felt a little more normal, as if he had imagined the energy-sapping effect in the first place, but he knew it had happened. He called out, "Ken, it sounds like you had a problem, and I'm sure you did the best you could. Why don't we get out of here and let me get you some help?"

"You still don't get it! I did it. I brought that guy here. He might not have figured it out without me. I caused it. I had to fix it. I couldn't let everyone die. And I couldn't let that guy go. I strangled him right there in that chair you're sitting in, with my belt, before he could stand up and fight me right. Then I burned all of his evil notes in that stupid case. His body is right behind you in the creek bed, under a ton of slate that I threw on him. It's over. I saved everyone, and nobody knows it. Now I have to do something with you." Ken produced a pistol from behind a rock and quickly moved to a crouched stance on the plank, pointing it at Jerry, with the falls down to the lake behind him.

Jerry jumped to his feet. "Whoa, Ken! Easy. You don't want to do this."

"You're not supposed to move. What's going on?" Ken stood up in surprise, slightly dropping his gun barrel. Jerry decided instantly that he had his chance and dove to his left for the shelter of a rock outcropping, unholstering his firearm as he jumped. Ken fired before thinking, striking Jerry in the upper right arm in an explosion of blood. Ken teetered for a moment, contemplating the mistake he had just made during the last seconds of his life, as the recoil energy from his gun tipped his six foot, four inch, skin-and-bones frame backward off of the plank and down the slate-lined falls, gravity smashing his skull on a four foot gray slab before the current swept his lifeless body rapidly to Mosquito Lake hundreds of feet below.

The next hours were a blur for Jerry: Using his belt as a tourniquet; Climbing up the steep embankment with the help of the widow Elizabeth who heard the gunshot and the subsequent yells for help from Jerry; The full speed drive with police lights on back the clinic in Haines; The flight to the hospital in Juneau; The flight from Juneau to Seattle for reconstructive surgery.

Days filled with sleep made the whole incident seem distant and unreal afterwards.

The next weeks that followed were filled with physical therapy during the days, punctuated with providing unofficial and official depositions and reports during the evenings. Jerry made several decisions during the period before returning to the Alaska. It was made very clear, repeatedly, that Jerry should refrain from talking about Dr. Kelly. Forever. He was told that there had been an investigation and the case was closed. Jerry never did learn where the guy came from, for whom he worked, or if any of the wild accusations Ken had claimed had any merit. Jerry was told to pretend that Dr. Kelly never existed and not to try to contact anyone about the case. Jerry decided to do just that. The second thing Jerry decided was that he had worked long enough as a Trooper and that it was time to let someone else, someone who would appreciate the job more, take his position. He was not sure what he would do for a living, but after living along the Haines Highway, and getting to know the people there, he was certain he would not be happy if he lived anywhere else. Finally, the last decision, the hardest, Jerry felt would be the most liberating. He decided that he would give up on his vision where he would be given a home if he would act as the caretaker of the Haines Highway area. He had tried, and he failed. He still believed the vision had been real. He would just now blame himself, not God, or the non-personal universe, for the broken contract.

God, if God existed, had made a decision too. When Jerry returned to Haines, he found that the deal of the vision had been resolved, in a personal, directed manner that was also a coincidence, seemingly. Jerry had been unceremonially returned his personal possessions from his office the day he visited to return his keys. Among "his" items was the metal case that had started it all. He had not made a report on the case, and being ordered never to talk about the incident again, he allowed all involved to believe that it was his. During one unemployed day in his small apartment, further examination of the metal briefcase reveled that the padding under the velvet-like material was actually created by just over three thousand $100 bills. Using a tax lawyer and employing a number of techniques that allowed taxes to be legally paid, Jerry eventually legitimized the money, gave half to Raymond anonymously, as he had agreed to do for fishing the case out of the water and turning it over to Jerry, and used the rest to buy Ken's house in Mosquito Lake across from the lucid dream inducing canyon that had been vacant since Ken's demise.

With the transaction complete, Jerry became the caretaker of the most important spot on the Haines Highway, the place where the execution by plague of most people on the planet had been diverted, the place that held a magic yet scientific power that could be used for good or evil. He owned his house free and clear, and spent his days fishing. And, caretaker Jerry lived happily ever after...

Fortune on the Chilkat River

"Would you go see what the Chief wants?" The darkness of the skin of the nurse's arm contrasted sharply with her white, starched uniform as she motioned at the call light control board in the nurses' station.

Dan didn't usually like dealing with the patient nicknamed "Chief" because of his dementia. Now that Chief was almost a hundred years old, he rarely used English when communicating. A nursing assistant like himself could spend half of a shift just trying to determine what it was Chief wanted when he used the call light. About the only English phrase Chief ever said was, "Your reward will come," which Dan could hear in his head already as he headed down the dark hallway of the nursing home to the man's room.

"What do you need, Chief?" Dan said as he entered the brightly lit, starkly furnished room.

Chief was sitting precariously in his wheelchair at a small desk with papers scattered about the floor. The side bedrail was still in the up position indicating to Dan that he had climbed over the rail and staggered to his wheelchair himself. Quite a feat considering his condition.

"Your reward will come!" stated Chief.

"Yea, yea. Look, you need to get back in bed." Dan proceeded to straighten up the papers on the desk. As he moved a rolled up parchment, a small leather hide bag tipped scattering a pile of rounded blue stones. "Wow! Chief, what are these?"

"Blue ones. I miss...oh, my blue ones," sighed Chief.

Dan examined the stones. They looked like sapphires. Sapphires? Was that what they were called? Dan was not an expert on stones, but he remembered how much of his paycheck Tammy had spent buying that ring with the blue stone on it before she left him. If these gems were the same kind, the pile of blue stones was worth a fortune, Dan surmised.

"So, uh Chief, where did you get these 'blue ones' anyway?" Dan inquired.

"I was a rich man. I saw blue ones for as far as a man could see," Chief gestured the horizon with his wrinkled curled hand. "It is a secret. Thousands. Everywhere. By the big egg rock. I am rich. Was... Secret. Your reward will come!"

Dan was impressed. Chief was never coherent, and never spoke so in English. Dan had rarely seen him so animated either. Obviously, the subject was pretty exciting to him. Chief began scattering papers until he had the yellowed sheet he was looking for. "My home," Chief said, holding the sheet. "Rich...land."

Dan grabbed the sheet. It was a hand drawn map. There was a town, a few roads, a river, and a little cove drawn with a small house on one side. In English, the word "Home" was written by the house. A few other words in Chief's native language punctuated the parchment. Dan showed the map to Chief and followed his light brown curled finger as he traced a line by the house picture up a hill to an egg shape surrounded by scores of little round circles. "*Hit xaatéen.* Blues. Your reward will come."

Dan understood at once. This was a treasure map. The kind of thing he had looked for all his life. A ticket to the good life. He looked at the map. The towns were marked. "Klukwan" and "Haines" were written in English. "You're from Alaska, right Chief?"

"Aaá."

"Is that yes, Alaska? Stay with me Chief."

"Yes. I am Alaska man."

"Thanks Chief, that's all I need to know. You need to get back in bed now." Dan grabbed the bag of blue stones and stuck them in his pocket. As he folded up the yellowed map, he felt a sharp pain in his arm. Looking, Dan was shocked. How could such a crippled hand be causing so much pain as it clamped his arm? "Back off Chief," Dan ordered as he pushed the arm away.

Chief would not let go. Sudden clarity possessed him. He was not going to let his last link to his home leave in the pocket of the honorless nursing assistant. With every last amount of being, he held on. "Your reward… WILL COME!" he shouted.

Dan at once became mad and scared. If he got caught stealing from the patients, he would end up back in jail, considering his record. He was not going back.

And he was not going to let go of this boon. This was his chance to make it. Suddenly, Dan's anger took hold. The anger that always seemed to ruin things in his life. But before he could think, Dan was watching his own fist launch out and strike the old man squarely in the shoulder. Dan could hear the bones under his fist snap as Chief flew off of his wheelchair to the floor, hitting his head on the steel bedrail.

Dan looked down at his work. Was the old man dead? No. Chief was breathing. But he was broken and bleeding. This was bad, and getting worse. Folding the map into his pocket with the blue stones, Dan ran into the darkened hallway and started screaming for the nurse. The next half an hour was filled with a rush of action that awoke the residents of the neighboring rooms. There were assessments, wound cleaning, followed by the clamber of the ambulance crew as Chief was taken away on the wheeled gurney to the nearest hospital. Dan repeated a story three times to the nurse for her records until she was finally satisfied. Chief had climbed over his bedrail and as Dan was helping him get back in bed, he slipped, hitting the floor and side bedrail. That was the official record now, so that was the truth. Dan was shaky, but he knew that he would never hear anything more about it. Chief just never talked in English, so no one would ever ask him about it. He felt bad. But soon, everything would look better. He had a treasure map. He was sick of the work in the nursing home anyway. Laughing as 7 a.m. came around, Dan knew that it would be the last time he would spend his life pacing the urine stained linoleum floors of the dank home for forgotten old people.

Dan awoke with a start. He was half falling off of a hard plastic seat. There were people walking all around him. He was in public. Where was he? Sitting up straight, Dan pulled the coat up that was acting as a blanket and strained to organize his thoughts. Yes, okay, he was on a ferry, that's right. Ferry. It seemed more like a cruise ship to him. Not like the ferry in Camas, that held one car and took one minute to cross the river. This was different. This was his chariot to his new life. But, after nearly three days, he was becoming sick of his new life filled with sleeping on the floors, smelling bad, having wrinkled clothes, and drifting around the ship decks like a bum. He should have spent an extra few hundred dollars for a cabin room. But he didn't have it. The blue stones he had hawked at the pawnshop had just barely given him enough money to pay for the tickets.

"Finally awake? Here, got you a coffee." Dan took the cup and looked at the disheveled young man with the uncombed hair and emerging beard. Dan hoped that he did not look as bad as his friend Pete who was offering the coffee.

"Dude, where are we?" Dan asked, taking a drink.

"We're almost there, next stop Haines. Whoo-hoo! Dude, I was just reading some stuff about Juneau, where they found all that gold. The dudes that found that gold had some Indian show them where it was. It's just like with you. Some Indian dude telling you where all that moo-lah is," Pete exclaimed excitedly, speaking loudly. Pete had displaced his usual bong hit and 40-ounce beer breakfasts with strong coffee and pastries during the trip. His newfound morning energy proved annoying to Dan.

"Shhh! Quiet! Man, you want to blow it? Some of these people might live there," Dan said as he grabbed Pete's arm for emphasis.

"Right, sorry man. I'll, uh, I'm going to go read some more stuff. We're almost there dude. Gonna be rich soon! Cheer up!"

Dan watched his "friend" meander off, allowing the rock of the ferry to exaggerate his swaying gait, making people move out of his way. What a jerk, he thought. I have got to get rid of him. It was as if Pete wanted to draw attention to himself, like he wanted to get caught. Dan didn't ever really like him, the mooch. He never worked or had any money to party with. But somehow he was always high or drunk. But he had a car, which was the main thing. Dan couldn't get a license for a few more years, of course. He needed Pete, or at least his car. The map showed that the treasure of sapphires was past the town of Klukwan in an area called "Ghuntéea" about 30 miles away from where the ferry landed in Haines. Dan had to have the car. He needed to lose Pete. Pete would do something stupid. Dan did not want to see what Alaskan prisons were like. Undoubtedly, they would be cold.

The loud speaker started in, with a garbled voice, indicating when people would be allowed onto the car deck. Dan had learned to tune out the announcements, as they were meaningless to him. The last three days had been a blur of endless pine trees and shorelines. The stops that were called towns were little more than a clump of houses around little taverns, which were always closed when the ferry arrived. But this stop was different. Dan gathered his coats and trash and became part of a line of tired travelers waiting for the painfully slow drift of the boat to stop at the dock. Pete bounded through awaiting families to find Dan, babbling about how he hoped he could find his car and how he hoped it would start. His comments were met with sighs from the apparent locals and new, worried excitement by the apparent newcomers to the ferry experience.

Despite concerns, the action flowed smoothly from the line, to the ferry deck, to the car, and then up the ramp to shores of Alaska. They had made it.

During the quick four-mile trip from the ferry dock to the town of Haines, Dan began to consider just where he was. Alaska. It was cold. August, summer, and it couldn't be warmer than 60 degrees outside. There was snow all around on the mountaintops. Was winter coming already? Was he going to stay until winter? He'd never make it. Looking at the trees, he wondered, were there really bears in there, like the movies showed? Probably not. He hadn't seen any on the shores while on the ferry. It was probably just Hollywood promoting the idea. But the mountains were astounding. Majestic jetting gray rock capped with snow. He never would have guessed that it looked this way from the map he printed off of the Internet.

"Is this the town? Look at it. Not much here. There must be more to it somewhere else," Pete mused as he kept the car paralyzed at the stop sign while he looked back and forth. Prompted by a honk from an RV from behind, Pete edged the rusty Buick down the hill.

"Dude, turn in there," Dan ordered, pointing to the log structure with the sign that read "Visitors Center." "I'll be right back. I have to find out where a town is."

"Find out if *this* town has a liquor store!" Pete shouted as Dan produced his stolen yellow map and entered the building.

Dan moved to the left once inside, away from the counter where an older couple were being shown colored pamphlets concerning flights over the local glaciers. Dan was first drawn to a large sled hung from the ceiling. A sign explained that the sled had been used in the movie *White Fang*, which had been filmed in the area. The small television played the movie as Dan moved about. One scene showed a large bear attacking a young man as he watched. He suddenly remembered being enamored by the movie one night after a late party. Would he need a dog sled to get to the treasure? He hoped not.

"Can I help you find something?" the voice came from behind the counter from a large smiling man. Dan and this man were the only two people left in the building, Dan suddenly realized.

"You live here right? Do you know where Ghunteéa is? It is by Klukwan, but I can't find it on a map."

"Yes," said the man, smiling. "That is the Tlingit name for a place now called Mosquito Lake or Moose Valley. That's where I live. Just go up the highway. It is at mile 27."

"Is that Highway 7, or Highway 1?"

"Well, there is only one road out of town. All the other roads end about ten miles out. So if you reach a dead end, you know that you took the wrong road, and you'll have to double back. As for the number, different maps have it listed differently. We call it the Haines Highway, or just *the* road."

Dan had to ask, "Are there really bears here?"

"Yes."

"No, really. You can tell me."

"There really are bears here. Just the other day I watched one eating the dandelions in my front yard. Here's a pamphlet that explains how to live with the bears." The smiling man produced a colored sheet as if it were a magic trick, without looking down while talking.

"Thanks. Mosquito Lake, huh, in the Valley of the Moose. I suppose it is by Bear Mountain on the shores of Salmon River," Dan jabbed.

Still smiling, the man replied, "Four Winds Mountain and the Chilkat River, which does refer to a vessel that holds salmon. This is Alaska…"

"Right," Dan said as he exited. For him, Alaska was the place to grab your fortune before returning to the civilized strip malls of Portland to spend the booty.

After stopping to buy a few 40 ounce bottles of beer to keep Pete quiet, the Buick was set on "the road" and the last leg of the journey was started. Thirteen miles out of Haines, Dan asked Peter to pull off near the river. Then he broke out the beer and toasted their accomplishments so far. Dan knew that this was a good time to get rid of Pete. It was not as he planned, but it had to be now. He couldn't risk Pete knowing where the treasure was. The situation was bad, but he'd come this far. He wasn't going to let this slob ruin his chance. Yes, that's it. Think of what a low-life this guy was, it would make it easier. Didn't Tom tell him one time that Pete stole some money from his room that one night? What a jerk...

"Dude, here's to gettin' rich in Alaska. A-ooh-haw!" Pete screamed loudly out the window and honked the horn.

"I hope that doesn't attract the bears," Dan said, truly worried about it. Dan allowed Pete to drink. He would be happy to sit all day and drink, if past experiences were any indication. From his pocket, Dan produced his surprise for Pete: a bottle of Yukon Jack 100 proof whiskey. Pete danced in his seat with the excitement of a child getting a train set on Christmas. For the next hour, Dan and Pete took turns taking long draws from the bottle. Dan used great skill in holding his tongue over the opening of the bottle and pretending to swallow, followed by hooting, while Pete used equal skill in taking two large swallows each time, while pretending to only take only one small sip. Soon, with most of the bottle gone, and his friend having difficulty speaking, Dan knew the time had come to say farewell to the jerk he had put up with long enough.

During the hour, Dan had imagined Pete as the cause of every bad thing that had ever happened in his life. Opening the driver's side door, Dan commanded Pete out to let him drive, so that Pete wouldn't end up in jail. Pete obliged, having to be held up by Dan.

"Dude, thanks. I don't want to go to jail... Dude, I love you," stammered Pete.

The rage that Dan had been building exploded. Pete, who was cursed with the ability to say or do the wrong thing at the wrong time, again fell victim to his own mouth. Dan screamed, "You're a fag! I knew it!" Dan swung the bottle in a long arc and slammed it into Pete's skull, making a loud pinging sound and spraying the car and Dan with warm blood. Dan stood over the crumpled body shouting as a small puddle of blood rolled towards the river. After several minutes, Dan calmed his breathing and examined the situation. This was bad. Dan felt ugly and evil. It had happened again. But, he had to keep his perspective, keep his eye on the prize, he thought. Pete was never meant to make it rich, he was doomed from the moment he put his feet on the ferry.

Without further hesitation, Dan grabbed Pete, threw him over his shoulder, and walked over the highway into the woods. Just like in the nursing home, he thought. Just another body, here one shift, gone the next. Dan stuck Pete behind a large rock, never checking to see if he was still breathing or not. Washing the blood off his face and arms in the bitterly cold silt-water river, Dan said aloud, "He's probably just drunk. He'll be fine after he sleeps it off. Unless the bears get him..." Dan shivered and looked back into the dark forest. He suddenly felt afraid. There really are bears in there, he thought. Within a minute, the Buick, with only a single passenger, was back on the road.

Fifteen minutes later, the sign that pointed to Klukwan had come and gone. Dan never saw the city itself, but he didn't need to. All he let himself worry about was the fact that he was about to be rich. A week ago, he was a Portland nobody. Now, he was just minutes away from having the good life. Over a bridge and around a bend, then without warning, Dan arrived at the Mosquito Lake road. He turned the car in and drove three miles to the end where he had to turn back. He never did find the town of Mosquito Lake, just a little store and a school, both closed. Returning back to the highway, Dan pulled over and examined the map.

Chief's map showed a little cove off of the river with a road next to it. That was where the house was, not really in the Ghunteéa, now called the Mosquito Lake area. The highway looked fairly new to Dan. He calculated that it probably had been built after Chief had moved. He continued up the highway slowly. One could tell where the highway had been built up and the riverbank had been changed to prevent flooding. Looking to the side, Dan suddenly saw an area overgrown, away from the highway, where the river had been at one time. The area looked like a cove, with a flatness that circled it that must have been an old road at a time before the highway.

Dan found a spot to pull the Buick into the forest. He then pulled a downed tree to cover the back end of the car. Convinced that it could not be seen from the road, he circled back on foot to the area he was now sure was the homestead pictured on the yellowed map. A little hill separated the area from the highway. Up close, it was obvious that the highway had been routed away from the cove to make an easy curve around the jetting mountain slope behind the area. Even though the three-foot high bright pink-flowered weeds were overgrown throughout the area, Dan could make out the footprint of a house area and a rough road. He found an old rusty box spring set among a scattering of gray square-shaped logs. "That's where the Chief made little Chiefs, I'll bet," Dan said out loud. The sound of his own voice shocked him back to a panic. I shouldn't talk, he thought. The bears might hear him. Get on with the work. Get the jewels out of the ground and get back to Portland, he told himself.

From the map and the way Chief had traced it with his finger, Dan could perfectly see where the path from the house to the mountain was. It was still there. A little grown over, but obvious, with the trees cut and the rocks and dirt packed. Bears be damned. This was it. Up the path to where the "blue ones" were. Riches awaited.

Dan followed the natural path for only a short distance before it became somewhat steep. There were loose white rocks that made climbing a little difficult. Dan began to consider if he had made a mistake following the natural path when suddenly he found himself in a flat wide clearing. It was as if a huge, wide-open stadium or theater had been carved out of the mountain. It was sunny, with bushes in all directions, but few trees. Then he saw it. A large, white, egg-shaped rock, just like Chief had said, just like on the map. This was it! He had found the treasure! All he had to do was pick up the thousands of sapphires, like the ones Chief had.

Dan looked about. He saw no blue stones. Just loose white rocks and dirt. He uncovered rocks. He dug in the dirt. Where were they? Did sapphires look differently in the wild? Maybe he should have researched the gems more. Panic set in. He dug. He covered every bit of the area, staring at the ground. Not a glint, not a fleck of any blue stone. Where were they? Chief said he was rich. This was the secret place, there was no doubt. But not a single stone, not a single "blue one."

Dan moved back to the edge of the hill. He looked down to see that yes, he had followed the path, just as the map directed.

Then, looking back to the egg rock he saw it. Blue. Yes blue. Blue everywhere. To the right, to the left, blue. A fortune in blue.

Blueberries!

Blueberries! Everywhere! The bushes were full of berries. A fortune! Not the fortune a modern nursing assistant from Portland would want. The kind of fortune a man living on his own in the woods of Alaska would covet. A fortune in berries. He screamed.

"Aaaaaaagg!!"

Everything he had done!

"Aaaaaggg!"

He had killed…for this…

"Nooooo!"

Suddenly he heard a scrambling in the dirt. Out of the corner of his eye, he saw movement in the bushes and something black rushing towards him. A bear, he thought. He must have called him by screaming. Quickly, Dan turned to run, but there was nowhere to go. He stopped and turned, then turned again. But before he could untangle his feet from the grasses and loose rocks beneath his feet, his body tipped sideways tumbling him over the edge and down the loose rock path he had climbed. Dan saw the black raven that had been the imagined bear fly past lazily, as his body hit hard, coming to rest in the high grass and weeds. He heard the crack of his upper back as it landed on a rock. He could see his chest pushed unnaturally high and forward as he looked up, hearing himself gasp. He could understand the impossible and vulnerable situation he now found himself in. But Dan could not move. His back was broken. His body was limp. Only his mind still worked.

Dan's mind raced. A silent scream filled his head. Panic. Fear. The taste of blood. A feeling of dizziness. Then a voice came to him, loud, clear, and inescapable. Throughout the next long two days and two nights, until the end of time, a single loud voice, of an honorable Tlingit elder rang out.

"Your reward will come."

"Your reward will come."

"Your reward will come…"

RETURN TO THE HAINES HIGHWAY

H is mood had been sour for many days. But he shouldn't complain. He was not in pain, and he and his family had been well-fed during the long winter. In fact, the sweet berries now, during the summer, had been some of the best he could remember. Sweet berries were one of the joys in life, and one of his most favorite rewards from the land. But, even the berries had not been able to lift his spirits of late. He was growing older, and he had reached the conclusion that he really did not like being around the people of his village at all times. He was the lone male bear, the name he took for himself, who needed space from others to be free. Space to be really alone was getting harder to get. Another, even worse fear, also gnawed at his thoughts recently, that soon, he will be too old to be away from people at all, and would have to stay in the village doing chores for his House in order to be worth a portion of the hunts or fish catches. The thought of needing to stay close to all those people, smeared with grease and smoke to keep the mosquitoes at bay, people, wanting to talk about this or that, people…It gave him a chill. He was Man Bear. He needed his own land.

Of course, Man Bear loved his family, and loved his village people. He would fight to the death simply to proclaim their right to exist in this new valley. And of course, his wife chose him over the man she was to marry because Man Bear was good, and would never abandon a wife or the House during this life. That love created the problem, and the source of his sour mood. He needed room to live. He hoped that being in the area that he had discovered where no people camped would refresh his drive. But it had done the opposite, and he mourned his future loss. He needed to think, to decide what was needed of him for both his happiness and the well being of his family and House.

When his clan decided to move out to where the New River valley met the ocean permanently, he had been very excited, and had actually been one who had insisted on the site. He had been traveling to the area for years to be alone, and knew of the secret that the New River never froze in the winter in one area. He had agreed that it was time to split the Houses to allow for more land for each group to gather meat and berries, and he imagined the riches that would follow from having a fresh water river that flowed all winter. In a generation, they would be one of the strongest families in all of the lands. But he imagined what would follow, that in the next years, the valley would be populated, and fish creeks and berry patches would be claimed for this mother or that grandmother. Soon, all of the private supplies of goodness that only he knew about would be lost by claim, and he would have to continually negotiate and associate with people, just to have what he already held alone. After the New River valley, there were no more good lands to run free in. He had explored the entire area, and after one or two days walk from where he was, the land turned to grass, with no trees, or was buried in long stretches of snow, even in the summer. This was all there was, and when it filled with people, his happiness would be gone.

"Chee-ya," a voice cried out, "Gee-a, gee-a." Man Bear jumped. People? Here? He stiffened, and then relaxed again. It was Raven, the trickster. Leaning back down, into the roots of the giant tree, he mused at the large black bird flapping his wings loudly, garbling in almost human tones as it exited over the low ridge. This small lake area where he rested belonged to the birds normally, and just like Man Bear, Raven probably bemoaned the upcoming intrusion of his people. Of course, Raven, knowing of his dilemma, had picked that moment to tease Man Bear with his voice. Even as a grown man, Raven was able to make him feel childish, and probably always would have such power. He thought briefly of the stories he had been told about the beings that had lived here before there were humans as he nibbled on some of the biggest berries he had eaten in years. In that time, Raven was said to be the keeper of the sun, although he had his doubts, as the sun seemed to be a very hot fire. He did not believe all of the stories exactly as they were told, especially after hearing his brother make up stories simply to scare children, but he admitted, he did not know about Spirits, the way others seemed to understand. It was best not to worry too much about such things that he could not change.

As the sun slipped behind the near mountain that still had snow at the peak, Man Bear surveyed the near surroundings for a camp for the short night. He was now a quick walk from the little lake, and to his side, a small stream for drinking flowed past a flat spot. The spot seemed familiar. He searched his memory for the locations of plants that would be close to supplement his next meals when he saw something glowing out of the corner of his eye. Instantly his mind raced: Fire! Coals! People! Bright light surrounded him in an instant. Only people brought light and fire. But it was not a fire, and the glow was the color of the tall pink flowers, not of the dark reds of coals. It was not a light made by a person. Whatever it was, it was dangerous he decided, and before he could think of what to do, Man Bear jumped down the small creek gully and hid silently behind a large tree. With any luck, he had reacted quickly enough that the creature that brought the light had not seen him, and he could wait for it to move on.

"It is just a bear... it is just *like* a bear," Man Bear told himself. He had been this close to countless bears, and he had always survived. "I will survive this time also."

As time passed, Man Bear's breathing slowed. Slowly, slowly, silently, he slid back up the little gully; always hidden, daring to sneak a peek between leaves at times. When he had moved back to within five or six arms lengths from the flame that was not a flame, he decided that he had positioned himself as close as possible, while remaining hidden and able to escape in a full run if needed. Terrified, yet excited, he watched closely the marvel that he had never imagined, and had never heard about, even in the wildest of stories or boasts. As the short period of summer semi-darkness descended on the forest, Man Bear studied, looking for clues, seeking a weakness, while the bright red-pink glow lit the ground and tree trunks, as if a magical, continual campfire had been erected for the night.

The glow of light appeared to be a misty cloud, as if fog. But unlike fog, the light had a definite shape. The light appeared to be a round, long pole, as if it were a perfectly straight and round small tree with no branches. The tree appeared to extend up far past the other treetops into the dark blue-black sky, and it appeared to continue into the ground, with no irregularities where one would expect roots to bulge out. The light glimmered and flowed within the pole with areas becoming bright, while other areas dimmed. The translucent, branchless, pink-red tree appeared to be in constant motion yet never changed shape while the surrounding trees and ground flickered. It became obvious that this was the work of Spirits, if not an actual Spirit itself. Man Bear became more and more certain as he watched that the light must be the handiwork of Raven, or at least something Raven would use to trick him or scare him from the area.

After what seemed an entire day, Man Bear decided that he could crouch and hide no longer. He was no child, and if this light had come to find him or test him, he decided that he needed to meet the challenge as a grown man and as a proud example of the courage of his House. In one motion, he jumped up to his feet and landed directly in front of the light, raising his hands above his head to appear as large as possible, and yelled loudly, "I am here, Raven!" Slightly shaking, as he stared directly into the shifting light pole, he could hear his words echoing throughout the small valley and to the lake and back. As there was no change, no reaction, he slowly lowered his arms. "I am here," he repeated, but at a conversational volume this time, suddenly considering with relief that the light might be a phenomenon not directed at him after all. Then, as if suddenly safe in his wife's arms, he collapsed to the ground to sit in front of the light to study it further.

The sky turned dark blue for a short time and began to gain light with morning returning before a single star could emerge, as the sun dipped for only a short period behind the mountain line. All the while, Man Bear studied the light sitting in the glow, nodding into sleep at times, transfixed by the rhythmic flowing pink-red patterns. With the increasing daylight gathering in the sky, the effect of the light was fading. Man Bear figured that it would be hard to see at all very soon. He had seen all that there was to see, he surmised, and decided that one last study was needed. Steeling his nerves, Man Bear stood, then reached out with his arm, and placed his left hand directly into the light. He had fully expected that his hand would be burned completely, as only fire can give light, and he braced for the pain. If he were to lose a hand, he wanted to keep his right hand intact, because the right hand was the important one, the one he had trained to hunt and fish. But Man Bear never felt any pain. He did not feel anything physically, until he opened his eyes and felt the sting across the front of his body that indicated that he had fallen flat to the ground on his face and chest.

Man Bear had not been burned, but he had been shown a vision by the Spirits that made the light, who had to be associated with Raven, he now had no doubt. There had been no words. He had been shown a story with pictures, and he simply knew what the story meant. The vision had been rapid, told in an instant, but somehow unraveled in his mind as if he were listening to a tale told by his uncle that lasted all through the night. Before he could move, Man Bear followed the story in his mind from beginning to end.

The land of the Spirits was also the land of his people and the valley where he now sat. The land was also all one big lake of stars somehow. The Spirits were alive like Man Bear and the animals, but in almost the entire big lake of stars, there were no people or animals. Somehow the moon and the stars that move in the sky had made it possible for animals to live here. The Spirits lived very far away from Man Bear and his people, and had been searching for a very, very long time for other people like himself. If the Spirits found no other people, all the Spirits would die, and the entire lake of stars would be empty forever. This would be very sad.

Man Bear could see the Spirits remembering two memories. In one memory, the Spirits searched forever for Man Bear's people and never found them, and everyone died. In the second memory, a clue had been left for the Spirits by a man, and the big lake of stars became filled with people and animals. The Spirits thought for a long time, then they flew the pink-red light to Man Bear. It was very hard because the land of the New River valley was moving and moving all the time, and it was very far away from the Spirits. It was also a long time ago, yet not somehow. The vision was confusing and made little sense, but Man Bear understood that it had been almost impossible for the light to reach him, as if the Spirits were fishing in the dark in the river with their bare hands. But they had found him. The Spirits wanted the one memory where the big lake of stars would fill with animals to become the true memory for all. It all depended on him. The Spirits implored Man Bear: You must do the thing that will give us the clue that you lived in the New River valley.

When Man Bear opened his eyes, the light was gone, the vision was over, and the forest looked bright and smelled sweet, as it always had. Everything was as it always had been. There were no signs on the ground where the light had been. The experience had been so unusual that his first instinct was to consider the whole experience a dream that could be ignored. But he was a grown man, and he would not deceive himself. He had been contacted and given a vision by the Spirits. It had been real. He was now very important to the Spirits, and he had been asked to complete a quest. He decided to accept his responsibility with courage to leave a clue for the Spirits to find later. But what did that mean? What would he do? Man Bear knew one thing: his old life was over. He had now grown past being an adult, the same way he had grown from a child to a man. Now he lived for the good of all people and the Spirits. He was no longer Man Bear. At once, he named himself New River Man. His life would be dedicated to filling his New River home with people. He vowed to show his people all the secrets of the valley he had learned, and hoped that his determination would provide the clues that the Spirits would need when they come.

New River Man spent many years watching two new generations of his people establish themselves large and strong Houses. He was a leader, always stressing the need for markers and signs to show the Spirits that this was their land and the good Spirits would always be welcome. When time finally wore New River Man to the point that his body could breathe no more, many hundreds of his people mourned his passage, and were proud that he continued to bring meat to the Houses until his last days without the need for assistance. Just before his body was taken to the deep woods to become part of the forest he loved, he imagined that the Spirits would be happy with him and would be waiting for him after he died. But the Spirits that he imagined and had met before were not even "born" when New River Man became a spirit in his own right. The Spirits that New River Man would met after death were different.

* *

"Wake up, John!" Abe whispered loudly.

"What is it, the still? Did it blow?" John yelled. Immediately his mouth was stuffed with a dirty wool mitt, gagging John with the smell and taste of rotten fish and sour whiskey mash.

"There's a light, an angel, come to visit us. I've been watching it for an hour," Abe continued his gruff whisper as John wrestled the hand away from his mouth and spit out the putrid taste. Even over the rotten fish taste, John could tell from Abe's breath that he had continued to drink too much moonshine after John had the sense enough to pass out, how many hours ago?

"Well, if it's been here an hour, why are you whispering?" John asked loudly, making Abe fall back and sit on his blanket on the frozen ground to try and deliberate the question. The hemlock trees spun slightly in front of Abe as he thought and tried to control his unfocusing eyes.

John was disoriented and mad. He had been happily warm and sleeping, a condition that was hard to come by in the untamed forest. He had had about enough of his drunken partner who had no control of himself. John was still quite drunk himself. There was no worse feeling, John remembered, than waking up already inebriated. All the fun of drunkenness disappeared when one awoke that way, and all that was left was confusion and stumbling. He took stock of his camp and became madder, as Abe lay babbling about angels and light. John's blankets all had snow in them, there were two empty bottles tipped by the supplies, which again cut into any profit they hoped to make for the work of the previous day, and the campfire and fire under the still were almost completely out. John tried hard to determine what else was wrong with the camp, but his head was spinning.

Suddenly John became shocked and sober. His heart actually jumped and pounded hard as it worked to regain a rhythmic beat, which caused him to fall back and join Abe on the ground. With the fires almost out, there should be no light in the camp at all. But all around them, a bright pink-red light blared, lighting up all the surrounding trees and the still. Ten feet away, emerging out of a large hemlock trunk about three feet from the ground, a long pole of light stretched to the sky, moving through branches as it moved up. John had seen light of this kind from ships or lighthouses, but he had never seen light go through object like trees, and he had never seen it of such a color.

"It's an angel!" Abe said, noticing that John was now aware of the situation. Abe staggered up to his feet, dragging most of the blankets further into the snow. "I'm – coming - for – you – angel," Abe continued, punctuating the words with each step, cutting a path in the snow towards the tree. Before John could untangle himself from the snow and clothes, and get to his own feet, with his balance still hampered from the repeated toasts a few hours prior, Abe had shuffled to the huge tree and grabbed at the pole of pink-red illumination. Silently, Abe reeled backward, burying himself in the snow on the ground, as the light disappeared. John stood staring, half dressed in the snow, cold, and trying to make out where Abe had landed, while his eyes adjusted to the dim red glow from the near-dead fires. John had all but resigned himself to the fact that Abe had electrocuted himself with the impossible light, and he would have to figure out how to dispose of his body. But when he finally reached Abe, he found Abe grinning and giggling. Abe never said a word of sense during the next half an hour of stumbling back to the campfire, getting wrapped up, and warming himself by the reignited firewood fire. By the time Abe was snoring loudly and John could finally relax back into his bedroll, he found himself entirely exhausted, with the alcohol in his bloodstream from the moonshine consumed just hours prior demanding that his body retire. Before he could relive the recent events in his mind, as unordinary and possibly dangerous as the situation might have been, he fell into an instant deep sleep.

When John reopened his eyes, the entire world was bright white, with the sun shinning from every surface in the snow-covered wilderness. Blinking repeatedly, he noticed that Abe had packed the entire camp except for the still, and was talking loudly to no one in particular, but obviously for the benefit of John, since he was the only person for miles.

"…And that's what I'm going to do, Jesus. I won't let you down. I know you could have picked a better man, but I am strong. I won't fail your charge…" Abe rambled as he tied his last pack tightly. "Mornin' John. We got to go and tell them."

John started slowly, reeling through the events of the night before in his mind, which seemed to him to be a disjointed bad dream. "What are you doin' Abe? You feeling good?"

Abe stopped, dropped his pack, pulled the large brim of his leather hat, slathered in oil to keep the rain out, down to his eyes, and stepped towards John, staring at him intensely. "I talked to the angels last night. They're in trouble. I got to do something. I got to do something to tell them I'm here. Jesus needs me..."

John realized at once that Abe had lost his mind. Maybe he hit his head when he was electrocuted. Electrocuted? What was that light anyway? It couldn't have been the Mounties, or they would be in jail. Hell, no one has a light like that, a light that goes through wood. "Abe, we are in the middle of making hooch here. Remember? Abe? It took forever to pack in all this sugar and get the yeast to grow all the mash with a warmin' stove. The boys in Porcupine and at the mine are waiting for us. Remember?"

"That light. The light told me what to do. The angels said that I got to make a sign for them. I'm sorry John, I got to go tell everybody."

"Whoa there, Abe. You ain't tellin' anyone about us. You are the one that keeps selling hooch in Klukwan. And you know as well as I do that ever since that Chilkat man went crazy drinking your whiskey and chewing on lupine root, it's been illegal to sell it there. Those Mounties already know what we are doing and they told me they would lock me up if they saw either of us again."

"Aw, Klukwan don't need me for hooch. They got stills all over town. I always get the blame, cause mine's the best. Got to double boil it," Abe grinned, making John feel better for a second.

"That's right, yours is the best, Abe. That's why I hitched up with you. So let's get back to brewing. You can't show your face around. We'll both end up in the work farm. I'm not goin' back. I can't."

"I'm sorry. I got to go. The angels told me. You keep the still. I'll tell them where to come to buy a bottle..."

"What? Now, you must have hit you head. You can't tell anyone what's going on. I can't let you leave." John was in a panic. He wasn't sure what had happened, and what was going on with Abe, but whatever it was, he couldn't let anyone find him here. And Abe knew that both Abe and himself were known by both the law in Haines and by the Mounties that kept an eye on the wilderness. He'd never make it in town. Plus, there were more than a few folks who would not feel bad about seeing their operation out of the way to open the market up for others. It was too serious. John felt for his rifle in the blanket.

"You take care. I'm taking a couple bottles for the shakes. You keep working the still," Abe said over his shoulder as he started away quickly.

John imagined Abe, drunk and crazy with his bottles, telling everyone about John and the still, and preaching blasphemies about angels and Jesus talking to him with light by the still. And then he remembered the work camp, and then imagined a mob of angry men. It was too much, too fast. What had happened?

"Stop! Stop Abe! Stop!" John shouted as Abe waved him off, not stopping or turning around. John's thoughts raced. Maybe he could get dressed, track him down, and then what? Break his legs? It was insane. What could he do?

Abe felt the jerk pull part of his heart meat through his chest and coat, and saw it flying in front of his eyes making the snow red before he heard the shot ring out behind him. Landing on his face, buried in the light snow, Abe managed to consider a few last thoughts in silence before becoming blind and deaf, and without ideas at all. He hoped that perhaps his death would be the thing that needed to be done. That thought made him happy. Perhaps, as Jesus had experienced, the angels simply told Abe that his life would end not in vain. That last happy thought remained as Abe died, expecting to see again the angels he met the night before. But the angels Abe met would be different ones, as the angels that Abe had met the night before were not even born when Abe exhaled his last breath.

* *

Tony toyed with one of the paperweights he had on his desk as he watched through his home office window the trees in the wind sway, blowing yellow leaves airborne. His paperweight collection was getting a little out of hand, he mused. He had so many clear Lucite blocks on his desk there was barely any room for his laptop and phone, the tools that allowed him to make a living from the depths of the Alaskan woods. Each Lucite piece held a story, being a present, a special thrift store find, and e-Bay treasure, etc. And each held an object, preserved forever, in a plastic prison, like a three-dimensional microscope slide for the eyes. Some held trinkets or coins, some held small statues of monuments or buildings. But the Lucite blocks that Tony coveted the most were the ones with living things inside such as a baby cactus or marine animal shells.

"Back to work," Tony said out loud, putting the block down and returning his attention back to the computer, paused in the middle of a scanned writing test completed by a high school student thousands of miles away. Not being able to secure a teaching position in the Borough because of the local politics, correcting tests online had become his new occupation, one that kept his wife and himself alive, but did little to cover all of the ever-looming bills. Living in the Haines Borough, with the same land size as Delaware State, but with only 2500 people and no industry other than fishing and a collection of minimum wage tourist guide summer jobs, one had to be retired or very creative to string together a living to survive. But Tony had reached the end of chances for creativity with his wife and with his creditors. He had agreed that he would be allowed only one more winter, and then, to save the marriage, they would move to Juneau for him to take a real job in teaching or with the government. Most likely, he would have to sell his beloved home in the woods. Tony vowed to enjoy every moment he had left in his Alaskan hideaway, and try not to think about the inevitable.

"Let's see, '*I want to attend college because...*i don't want to go to no college. Cause scool is stupit i only taking this test cause they make me do it wich is stupit two'," Tony read aloud with a sigh. These types of responses amused him in the past, but after reading over a hundred similar essays, with almost predictably identical misspellings and errors in grammar, they now just bored him. It must be the fact that high school students spend most of their time text messaging that leads to such similarities. How sad, Tony considered, that some teacher's livelihood and job depends on how well this student scores on her test, when the student obviously never had any intention of trying to present a proper response. He half considered giving the student a stellar score for the imaginary teacher's sake, knowing that no one else would ever see the test again. But, he couldn't chance it. He needed what little money the job offered, as his wife was half-packed as it was, being tired of living in the wilderness without modern luxuries.

Forcing himself to wade through the test essay scoring parameters, Tony picked up another clear paperweight with a thimbleful of straight needles encased inside and stared back out the window at the blustery afternoon playing out in the 3 acres of Mosquito Lake "town" on the Haines Highway that he claimed as his. If only they could keep up the payments. It was hard to think of Mosquito Lake as a town, having moved from "down south," as Alaskans say. In reality, it was simply a three-mile road turnoff from the Haines Highway to the natural little lake with houses and cabins tucked here and there along the way. But that was the way he liked it, alone with his wife and free to do what he wanted without worrying about prying eyes. Hopefully, something would work out and he could keep his sanctuary of solitude.

The shadows from the large swaying spruce branches created a strobe-like effect in Tony's office with his lights being turned off. The sun blinking between the swaying branches made the paperweight alternately change in color from blinding white to green, reflecting the color of the near books on the shelf. As he watched, the color changed, alternating from white to bright pink-red, which was captivating for a few moments. After a little while, Tony wondered what would create such a pink color, looking about his office first before turning his gaze outside. It didn't take long for him to see the pole of light the color of fireweed flowers emerging from his greenhouse in his yard, just twenty feet from his office window.

Immediately, Tony ran out of his house in his bare feet and stopped stammering at the door of the greenhouse. Extending from the wood frame roof was a long stream of light about the diameter of a six-inch drainpipe that went into tree branches above without being blocked as the wind blew limbs in the path of the light. Tony could see the light hit the wood frame of the greenhouse roof and continue through into the greenhouse, through a large planter box filled with dirt and emerge to continue to the floor. It looked like a huge fireweed-colored laser pointer focused down at his greenhouse, but one so powerful that it burned right through solid objects without damaging them. He strained his view upward. Was it a satellite? Or was it the International Space Station, conducting an experiment? Maybe this is the way they make crop circles, Tony considered. But who were *they*? And how the heck do they get light to pass through wood? He had just read about how the Navy bundled six metal-cutting lasers used in making cars parts together, and aimed it at and brought down drone aircraft. Was this another military test? It was nuts, whatever it was, he decided. Whoever was at fault, they sure missed their target, unless they thought no one lived in these woods, which was possible, Tony continued in his mind, still standing in a frozen stance in the chilling wind in short sleeves and bare feet. Mosquito Lake is one of the only places in the nation that does not have cell phone capabilities, and therefore, a place without people to accidentally laser to death, a low-paid government clerk might have concluded during a preliminary targeting assignment about which he had no concern.

Tony entered the greenhouse, partly to get out of the wind. Inside, the light looked like a huge pink-red florescent light tube attached from the dirt to the wood of the ceiling. In similar fashion to a glass tube, it appeared to be a vessel for some kind of swirling gas inside that promoted the light to emit. "It's impossible," he said aloud. He knew that light could not pass down through wood, or up through dirt, for that matter. What could he do? He could call the one State Trooper for the Borough. But that would take at least a half-an-hour for him to get here, if he would want to come out at all to see a light. He could find his wife to show her. But that would just add to her argument that they needed to move to Juneau or Anchorage where they could both work, this house being targeted by lasers. Maybe he could film it. Tony wondered if his little video recorder would even make out the semi-translucent brightness. But then what? Youtube?

While considering his options, Tony absent-mindedly reached out to see how the light would reflect off of his hand, thinking still that the light was similar a light created by the laser pointer he used to play with his cat. The instant his hand touched the light edge, everything went black, and the next time Tony opened his eyes, he realized that he had slumped on his side, leaning against one wall of his greenhouse with his arm pinned on a shelf, which kept him from falling completely to the ground. From the amount of throbbing in his arm that had "fallen asleep," Tony estimated that he had been unconscious for at least a few minutes. The light was gone, but the wind continued, rattling the plastic sheeting of the greenhouse with large yellow cottonwood leaves.

Tony immediately remembered a vision, a long story or dream that had just occurred. It was much more than a dream. It was a detailed movie involving him. But it was a strong memory also. It really had happened, somehow, but obviously could not have really happened, to his body at least. It certainly was powerful, Tony understood, as he worked his mind back through what he had just been shown.

Tony was shown big concepts without words. He was shown pictures and understood instantly what they were and how they connected to each other. Whenever he felt that he didn't understand a point, the picture would expand into other pictures until all aspects made sense. For example, he was first shown a galaxy. Tony thought to himself, "Which galaxy is this?" and then he was made aware that it was his galaxy, the Milky Way, and then he was shown Earth's position and the position of the star of the beings making the vision for him to see. The system was elegant and immense. Tony realized that as he sat in his greenhouse remembering what he had been shown, the vision was expanding more and more, becoming a larger version than he had originally experienced. "Magical," the whole experience was now evolving into for Tony.

Tony was shown that the entire three-dimensional universe, everything that existed, was merely an experiment by greater beings that could only be considered God. The universe was continued with some amount of effort and was in danger of being discontinued from existence. The ending of the universe was not as Tony would imagine, but would be extinguished from time itself, with the result being that the entire universe will have never existed in the first place. If that happened, both the Milky Way and Earth would have never been created. The "Eldest" or "Oldest People," as they called themselves, had created the pink-red light that Tony had seen. They were able to learn the knowledge about the nature of the universe through a certain way of "seeing" alternate timelines that could exist and through the discovery of a method of communicating with similar energy-based life in other galaxies through breeches in time-space that Tony was shown, but completely baffled by, having no frame of reference. In order to continue the universe, God required that life exist throughout. Life, especially complex life capable of knowing that it was alive in three-dimensions, provided God a unique power somehow, in a way unmeasurable to three dimensional creatures, that was valued highly. Each galaxy, being trapped to its own confinement due to the immense distances between them, had to rely on its own resourcefulness to ensure that life thrived in as many areas as possible to please God. Tony was shown that in our Milky Way, only the Eldest had the knowledge and technology to attempt to fulfill this universal directive. That technology had led them to communicate with him.

Tony was shown that throughout the entire Milky Way, life was very rare. What simple cells that might arise in promising condition were constantly destroyed by the ever-changing nature of space. Only a very specific set of five conditions ever really created the complex type of life desired. First, a planet or similar object was required that had moderate gravity and constant temperatures that allowed for liquids to collect in large volumes. Second, an additional source of pulsating gravity, such as a large orbiting moon, or small star was required to agitate and mix the liquid constantly. Third, the planet must have a liquid iron core that creates a magnetic field around the planet to shield the radiation emitted by all suns and stars. Fourth, the planet must be part of a system that has larger planets in close orbits that sweep with gravity all of the rouge asteroids and comets out of the area to allow enough time between planetary bombardments for life to form. And lastly, life formation requires luck and time.

Complex life formation in the Milky Way was very, very rare.

Tony watched as he saw the Eldest search and search endlessly, for millennia, combing planetary systems for a planet that could be the source for galaxian life. Compared to the billions upon billions of ever-changing planets, the resources of the Eldest were minute. Their population was spread extremely thin, with single excursion searches taking hundreds of years at a time, distances between stars being so tremendous. All attempts to modify their own life form or increasing procreation had failed because of their energy form condition and something intangible about the hidden element of life that they could not reproduce artificially. In fact, their experimentation had resulted in a mistake that changed an element that was "inherited" that allowed for intelligence in their species. In time, they would become extinct, unless the opportunity for modification and combination with a new life form occurred. The Eldest endlessly searched, for the sake of their own future, and for the sake of the universe itself.

Tony saw how the Eldest would search far distances by calculating huge formulas concerning spins of planets, orbits of suns in the galaxy, and effects of reaching back through time as they tried repeatedly to find by chance an exact spot on an exact planet at an exact moment in time that would reveal life. The probing for life took the form of long fingers of light that reminded Tony of the fireweed colored light that had entered his greenhouse. Finally, Tony was shown how his own planet would be probed in the future, at one specific place on the surface, and that the probe would show that the planet was barren, without life or evidence that there had ever been life. After that, the Eldest would continue their search elsewhere, but eventually would die as a race. The Milky Way would become empty, with no life of any consequence continuing, and would end in helping promote the eventual demise of the universe itself, being of no value to God.

Tony watched in his mind the Eldest use their powers to examine alternate forms of the Milky Way, based on events that could have happened in the past that would have changed the present and future outcomes. The individual Eldest involved in such work eventually went insane and died, but many volunteered to find a different past that would lead to a populated galaxy. After many years, a single timeline was discovered in which some sentient creature, on a planet extremely distant to the Elders, did one action that allowed the Elders to discover life on that planet in the future. That future discovery in the alternate timeline would in turn allow for an excursion back in time from a distance Eldest explorer who, by chance, lingered from their home planet before their demise. Because of the proximity, that Eldest ship would send a probe that would press the limits of time reversal to collect the discovered life and spread it to every corner of the Milky Way.

The Eldest worked again for years, and dedicated much of their planetary resources to create a messenger probe that could traverse back through time to try to promote the change in history and the timeline that would result in their discovery of life. There was extreme difficulty in establishing the exact directional formulas that allowed the Eldest to send a message to the exact spot on the planet where the future life-searching probe would examine. The message probe needed to repeat throughout the past, at exact locations and times where the planet had been, plus it had to be in a style and form that would attract and convey a message to sentient beings of limited intelligence no matter what their form might be.

After Tony understood the history that had led to his discovering the light and the vision it provided, an overpowering sense of urgency overwhelmed his mind and body. He saw in his mind the Eldest, all of them in one voice, begging him, commanding him, praying for him to do something. They begged: Do that one thing that tells us you were there. Tony's eyes were open, he knew he was in his greenhouse, but he also had foremost in his mind, the Eldest and their need for his action. He needed to do *it*. But what was it? That thing that told everyone that he was here, in Mosquito Lake, on the Haines Highway, on the planet Earth at this time, in the Milky Way galaxy, in the three-dimensional universe, in the experiment lab of God. As he stood up, straightening the tipped-over tomatoes cages, he thought, "Now how am I going to do that?"

The next years were a blur for Tony. He and his wife had made plans to move to Juneau for work after the snow melted. But Tony had become frantic over the long winter months, being trapped indoors by the eight-foot standing snow. In the past, he had loved winters, with the need for nothing more than to stay safe and warm, chopping wood and watching the stars during the practically endless nights. Since the commands of the Eldest, Tony felt the need to do something; only he could not determine what that something was. Tony's wife had survived the freeze-in with grace. She was pleasant and calm, but had decided that Tony had clearly lost his mind, and learned to think of other things with her eyes glazed over when Tony started into his nightly tirades about his need to save the galaxy. She tried repeatedly without success to take Tony to see the doctor in Haines. Tony grew increasingly homebound, and refused for weeks on end from leaving sight of his house. Once, she called for an ambulance to haul him away. One of the neighbors came to the house, as a medical first responder, and he and Tony talked about local gossip for forty-five minutes before the neighbor politely told her to reserve calling for medical help in extreme emergencies only, grumbling about having missed his dinner. By May, it was obvious to his wife that Tony had no intention of moving to Juneau, and she decided that she could not be a part of his quest to save the Eldest, a race of aliens she had grown sick of hearing about.

At first, being alone made Tony feel that he was making progress. He was allowed to concentrate on doing the thing he needed to do without having to explain himself all the time. But soon, he developed a need to talk to himself while he worked, and only in partial sentences, with part of the speech being said in his head. This habit tended to alienate all the friends

Tony had made over the years, and made it hard for him to receive assistance when he needed it. Tony never left his home, for fear that he would miss his opportunity. He had all of his food sent to him in the mail, charging everything on credit cards. Work had become an impossibility, and paying bills had become a game of shuffling money from one credit card or line of credit to another, occasionally paying off bills with money earned from selling his worldly possessions one at a time on e-Bay. Eventually, after two years, the burden became insurmountable, and financial pressure mounted to the point of driving Tony into rages of panic and mania, not knowing where he would turn for the very food he would need to continue his vigil at his house, which was the center of all hope for the galaxy, an importance no one seemed to understand.

Tony had attempted many projects that might lead to the Eldest discovering his existence in the future. Many seemed silly, but he had to try something. That is what they demanded, and continued to demand each time he closed his eyes. The first summer, Tony spent considerable energy constructing a one-story pyramid out of granite stones behind his house. He decided that it was a good start, as the pyramids in Egypt had shown modern people the existence of an ancient society after thousands of years had passed. In similar fashion, he forged a cave of large rock slabs, on which he chiseled detailed stick figure scenes describing in pictures the plight of the Eldest. He could never tell if he had done enough, and he was never sure if he were missing some obvious action that he should had done. After years, his property surrounding his house became a collection rock temples and small collections that only made sense to Tony, which spurred rumors throughout the Borough that he had lost his mind and was forming a cult along the Haines Highway.

By the third year since being shown the vision of the Eldest, Tony's existence had evolved to become a mere shell of his former life. His house was practically empty, save his aging laptop computer, his yard and rock tools, and his collection of Lucite paperweights that he could never bear to part with. He had no social life. He had also given up sleeping, tending instead to sit and stare at the greenhouse for long hours at a time, hoping for the return of the fireweed flower colored pink-red light, and some new directives from the Eldest. But the light never returned. The only messages he received were the stream of overdue bills and the ever increasingly threatening eviction notices, which Tony never took seriously being that his house was in the wilderness of Alaska and the bank threatening was located in New Jersey.

It was the first day below freezing that September when the two large vans pulled up to Tony's house. They were not from Haines, nor even Alaska, as far as he could tell. Refusing to show himself to the crowd of men with clipboards and tools by hiding in the empty upstairs bedroom, Tony endured a full hour of knocking and yelling, as notices were nailed to doors and siding all around the house and garage. Using a bullhorn, the men informed Tony that he had one day to "evacuate the house and surrender the keys." It was promised that he would be removed by force if the need arose. Then they disappeared. During the next hour that Tony sat in silence before he dared exit the bedroom, Tony had decided what last action he needed to take, and hoped that it would be enough for the Eldest, as he was out of options.

Tony surmised that if he allowed his home to be repossessed, new owners would eventually take ownership and undoubtedly undo and clear all of the work he had done to leave clues for the future. Without haste, he worked through his last night at home to make his land as unlivable as he could. Breaking the front axle on his old jeep, Tony managed to rip out his well, pull up the electrical transfer lines and box, and bulldoze the driveways impassable. Emptying the last remnants of the heating oil from the house tank, Tony splashed every surface of the garage and house making him dizzy from fumes as he waited for 3 a.m. to start the fireworks, the hour he surmised that would elicit the slowest response to attempt to quell the fire. He dressed with several layers of his outdoor clothing, packing his sleeping bag and all the food he could carry in a pack by the door. His plan was to camp in the woods as long as he could, and spend the rest of his life protecting his land and scaring away potential buyers by making the area unlivable.

Tony wasn't sure what had ignited the house prematurely, something with a remaining static charge after he had pulled the wires to the house out, or perhaps some chemical reaction, but it caught him by surprise how quickly flames spread to every corner. Quickly taking one last glance around the house that was becoming a memory as he looked, Tony noticed the glint of the one set of items he couldn't bear to see disappear. Grabbing quickly, he filled the two large front pockets of his coat with his beloved collection of paperweights, suddenly taking note of the heat blasting his uncovered face and hands. Running out of the front door with his collection and pack, Tony was both relieved and extremely disheartened to see his world transform into walls of yellow and orange, and billowing smoke. He stood transfixed and watched his beloved sanctuary become one huge flame that reached above the treetops for several moments before the pain hit him. Sheering, explosive, covering his entire back, Tony realized at once that his old life was over in a more final manner than he had planned for. Grabbing frantically for the zipper and buttons, he involuntarily screamed loudly the death cry that only a human experiencing a pain signal from every nerve end can produce. Managing to remove his outer layer, Tony's pain spread forward, engulfing legs and chest, and finally face. Relievingly losing consciousness as his screams echoed back from the mountains and lake, he fell to the ground, never to awaken again. Tony's prized Lucite encased treasures scattered on the grass with the last fling of his coat, only to be buried into the soft ground by the heavy rubber boots of the Klehini Valley Volunteer Fire Department fireman as he worked to try to revive and transport the mostly burned corpse. None of the firemen knew their transport had been the holder of the biggest responsibility in the galaxy before that day.

* *

The Eldest continued the galaxy survey. From the viewpoint of Earth, a single finger of bright light appeared at once touching the surface at the point of land that had once been named the Haines Borough of Alaska by the complex, multi-cellular creatures that lived there. Being connected through an unseen dimension of space over a distance half the length of the Milky Way, the probe of the Eldest actually had no substance or light. Even light would have made the apparatus infinitely massive. The probe did glow, made from part of the hidden "black" matter that comprised most of the three-dimensional universe, a material that reacted with gravity to form light when it was captured in the manner the Eldest used to gather information at such impossible distant distances.

The probe of the planet had held a level of hope for success that made it slightly more important than the previous one hundred or so planet surveys. The initial sector scrutiny flagged the star system because of the temperate proximity to the star, the presence of larger planets, and what had been recorded as possible liquid water. But as soon as the probe data transferred, it was obvious that the planet was yet another example member to be added to the endless analysis of a dead celestial bodies. There was no planetary atmosphere or sign of water moisture. The surface was covered by fine layers dust with radioactive traces. The star's activity had scoured the planet surface relentlessly, precluding the chance of finding clues of past life, if any had managed to squeak out a short existence at one time on the inhospitable ball. The probe results were conclusive: No life. Once recorded, the finger of light disappeared, with no further intelligent activity occurring on the planet surface once known as Earth until the planet dissolved and was absorbed by the expansion of the dying star once known as "Sun," four billion planetary orbit revolutions later.

* *

So-lat and So-leew had been picked by lottery, as was the Eldest custom, and power to control was transferred to their energy patterns. It had been many years since the alternate timeline and history had been identified, and the consent had been unanimous that the change to the past was to be attempted. Only a few times had there arisen a need so great that there was a call to change the timeline, but once decided upon and set in the controlling complex planet, the actual command to start the action was given to a random pair of Eldest citizens. The pair were separated from the population to start the process at the time of their choosing, to hold the personal responsibility of the chance that they would destroy everything known in the past, and to be the last failsafe for consideration of the need for such a drastic action. Changes to the past timelines resulted in a momentary disorientation, it was said, as the present three-dimensional time/space merged with another. But not even the Eldest were sure. Once changed, history was perceived as being as it always was. By giving the power to start the history changing process to individuals as was customary, the population could not anticipate the moment of change, or even be confident that a change had ever occurred, once completed.

So-lat communicated via pulsating excitement of the thick atmosphere to So-leew, explaining to So-leew that it had determined that it was willing to attempt the timeline change as it agreed the change was necessary. So-lat illuminated the first control.

So-leew responded in the pulsating communication that could be translated roughly as, "I concur So-lat. This must be the time. I am honored to serve the Galaxy in this manner, and I must comment that I have enjoyed our time together. Perhaps we can serve on an expedition together in the future, however this change turns out."

"Things may not change at all. I understand that the mathematics are so complex that the message probe to the past may have such difficulty staying connected to the small target area on the planet half the galaxy away that it will be very intermittent," So-lat worried openly. "Plus the message itself may be impossible for material-based life to comprehend."

"We have done what we can. Perhaps it shall be proof enough of our worth to the Creators of the Universe." Hoping the action would be best for So-lat, who had already started the message probe release process, So-leew illuminated the final control without warning, launching the message probe back to the past.

So-lat and So-leew would never sense and action occurring from completing the launch sequence, as it was launched backwards through time, through the imperceptible forth dimension of space to arrive at countless locations of space and time, many instances shared with the planet Earth of the past. If one could go back in time and watch the visual effect from space, one would see the thinnest flicker of a pink-red hair spear one spot on the planet at times, rotating in direction with relationship to the spin of the planet, orbit of the planet around the star, and movement of the star as it rotated about the Milky Way. The occasional flicker would resemble the effect produced by the ions from the sun getting caught in the planetary magnetic poles causing the Borealis, and would most likely be ignored by any non-advanced population.

"Did you feel something?" So-leew asked So-lat, flipping the tail of her mammal body now attached to her energy pattern.

So-lat considered, then replied, "I still feel sensations that are difficult not to react to. But it is getting better. This bird body is fourth generation, and I just stabilized the chemical energy requirements. It is amazing how much solid matter a body requires each day just to keep all the systems functioning properly." So-lat flapped his long black wings, admiring the large feathered creature that his energy pattern was now a part.

"I rather enjoy the consumption of solid energy part myself. A great variety of plant life is available now that larger series of transports are arriving. The number of planets seeded with life is becoming practically exponential ever since it has become the primary activity directive of the Eldest. Soon the number of modified and accelerated adaptations of the original life forms will be able to populate every star group in the galaxy." With that thought, So-leew felt an overwhelming wave of happiness and satisfaction.

What luck, So-leew thought, that the Eldest have had. For some inextricable reason, some intelligent animal on one distant rock of a planet halfway across the galaxy had encased complex life samples in a small, hard, resistant, clear material for preservation and presentation. And by chance, in only one area on the planet, where a single distant probe would analyze, the preserved life samples were placed for display, at the surface, preserved in clay rock. Once found, it was just a matter of happenstance and directed resources to secure cellular samples from the past from an incredibly large treasure trove of variable life, all based on an amazingly simple yet sophisticated method for protein replication that results in innumerable forms, all of which holding the intangible essence, valued as life.

So-leew had been told that attaching her energy pattern with the corporeal form would result in emotional changes, a complication she accepted as did most Eldest for the good of the Universe in the quest for procreation and research. But So-leew had not anticipated how good it would feel. She felt powerful and excited. Just happy to be alive. It felt good to be alive. She decided that the feeling must be related to the intangible aspect of life that energizes the Universe and makes it valuable, and valued. So-leew was grateful to be sharing her existence and this feeling with all that was. Silently, she personally thanked everything in the universe and beyond: All that had happened allowing the galaxy to exist, all that had acted to create the events that led to her living in that moment, and all that allowed her to know what it meant to be happy. She hoped that somehow, the Creators of the Universe could feel her inner thoughts and appreciation.

* *

The Beings that existed beyond comprehension were pleased. The valuable three-dimensional universe experiment was allowed to exist.